W8-CDW-069

9/28 50¢

Sydney Bryant is back—and it's a welcome return! Her fans and new readers alike are going to
admire how this classy, competent investigator
handles her second baffling case."

DEADLY GROUNDS

The sky was darkening fast. Nicole tried to make
out the lights of the main building through the
trees, but couldn't. Even so, she took comfort
knowing that, whether she could see the school or
not, it was only a few hundred yards away.

She walked on. The scent of acacia vied with
eucalyptus and she wrinkled her nose.

There was another smell, she realized then, a
sharper smell that she couldn't quite place, but
which for some reason made her uneasy.

Ahead, she could see that something was partially blocking the path.

Another step, and the shape took form.

It was a she, and she was wearing, Nicole could
see now, the familiar dark plaid skirt and white
blouse that served as the school uniform. The
blouse, however, wasn't white any longer.

Nicole closed her eyes then, not willing to
recognize the girl, but it was already too late. She
knew who it was.

"Oh, God," she whispered, and her hand flew
up to cover her mouth . . .

ZEBRA'S GOT THE FINEST
IN BONE-CHILLING TERROR!

NIGHT WHISPER   (2092, $3.95)
by Patricia Wallace
Twenty-six years have passed since Paige Brown lost her parents
in the bizarre Tranquility Murders. Now Paige is back in her
home town. And the bloody nightmare is far from over . . . it has
only just begun!

TOY CEMETERY   (2228, $3.95)
by William W. Johnstone
A young man inherits a magnificent collection of dolls. But an
ancient, unspeakable evil lurks behind the vacant eyes and
painted-on smiles of his deadly toys!

GUARDIAN ANGELS   (2278, $3.95)
by Joseph Citro
The blood-soaked walls of the old Whitcombe house have been
painted over, the broken-down doors repaired, and a new family
has moved in. But fifteen-year-old Will Crockett knows something is wrong—something so evil only a kid's imagination could
conceive of its horror!

SMOKE   (2255, $3.95)
by Ruby Jean Jensen
Little Ellen was sure it was Alladdin's lamp she had found at the
local garage sale. And no power on Earth could stop the terror
unleashed when she rubbed the magic lamp to make the genie appear!

WATER BABY   (2188, $3.95)
by Patricia Wallace
Her strangeness after her sister's drowning made Kelly the victim
of her schoolmates' cruelty. But then all the gruesome, water-re-
lated "accidents" began. It seemed someone was looking after
Kelly—all too well!

*Available wherever paperbacks are sold, or order direct from the
Publisher. Send cover price plus 50¢ per copy for mailing and
handling to Zebra Books, Dept. 2653, 475 Park Avenue South,
New York, N.Y. 10016. Residents of New York, New Jersey and
Pennsylvania must include sales tax. DO NOT SEND CASH.*

DEADLY GROUNDS

PATRICIA WALLACE

ZEBRA BOOKS
KENSINGTON PUBLISHING CORP.

ZEBRA BOOKS

are published by

Kensington Publishing Corp.
475 Park Avenue South
New York, NY 10016

Copyright © 1989 by Patricia Wallace Estrada

All rights reserved. No part of this book may be reproduced
in any form or by any means without the prior written
consent of the Publisher, excepting brief quotes used in
reviews.

First printing: May, 1989

Printed in the United States of America

Hearts live by being wounded.
                              Oscar Wilde

PROLOGUE

"Nicole? Did you hear me?"

A hand came to rest on her shoulder.

Startled, Nicole Halpern blinked and looked up from her chemistry textbook.

Miss Shanfield, the school librarian, was peering at her sternly through wire-rimmed glasses, and shaking her head. "Honestly, I wonder about you girls sometimes."

Her mind still occupied with memorizing the formula for perchloric acid, Nicole hadn't the faintest idea what—or who—the librarian was referring to.

"Girls?" Nicole said, and glanced around; the aisles were deserted, and there was no one else in sight. When had Terri and Melanie left?

"Trying to cram a full semester of study into the week before finals." Miss Shanfield made a sound of disapproval. "In my day, a young lady whose family circumstances were such that she was fortunate enough to be able to attend a private

7

school like Hilyer could be counted on to make the very most of the opportunity to learn."

She *had* been learning until she was interrupted, but Nicole knew it wouldn't do to say so. Instead, she murmured, "Yes, Miss Shanfield," while trying to appear properly chastened.

"Yes, well." Miss Shanfield sighed and turned back towards the checkout desk. "What I meant to say, was, I'm about to close the library, and you'd best be off before it gets dark out."

A quick look at her watch showed that it was a few minutes past eight.

Was that possible? Eight o'clock?

She'd come straight to the library after her last class let out at ten to three, intending to study until six or so. Since her father was out of town on business and she was boarding on campus while he was away, she'd planned to have a light dinner in the freshman-sophomore dining hall before going up to her room for a few more hours of reading.

But the dining hall closed at seven. She'd missed dinner, light or otherwise.

How had the time gotten away from her?

Eight o'clock.

In June it didn't get fully dark until eight-thirty or so; but the eucalyptus, acacia, and pepper trees, which during the day shaded the winding pathway between the library and the main building, also hastened twilight beneath an overgrowth of branches after the sun set.

On a moonless night, or when the fog rolled off

the ocean, rumor had it that it could get pretty spooky walking the path alone . . .

Thank goodness, I don't go in for *that* kind of nonsense, Nicole thought.

She marked her place in her chemistry book, closed it, slid it into her backpack, and began collecting her notes which were scattered all over the table. For a moment she thought she'd lost the lab workbook Melanie had loaned her—it was irreplaceable, Melanie would kill her for sure— but then she found it tucked between her history and English texts.

When everything was crammed into the backpack, she hoisted it onto her left shoulder, peeked under the table to make certain none of her notes had fallen to the floor, and started towards the door.

Miss Shanfield was using a pencil eraser to page through a small stack of papers. "Good night," the librarian said, without looking up.

"Good night."

The sprinklers had been turned on, and the mechanism whirred as the pulsing water arced across the thick green lawn and splattered on the stone walkway. Beads of water collected on blades of grass and glistened in what little light shone from the library windows.

The sky was darkening fast.

Nicole slipped her right arm through the strap to distribute the weight of the backpack more evenly, then started down the path.

Unbidden, the melody from *Peter and the Wolf* began to play in her head.

"Wolves," she said aloud, and fell silent. She'd meant to laugh at her own silliness, but her voice didn't sound right, and she didn't want to hear it.

She tried to make out the lights of the main building through the trees, but couldn't.

Even so, she took comfort knowing that, whether she could see the school or not, it was only a few hundred yards away at the most.

She walked on.

A light wind had come up and the branches of the trees rustled, seeming almost to whisper as she walked beneath them. The scent of acacia vied with eucalyptus and she wrinkled her nose.

There was another smell, she suddenly realized. A sharper smell she couldn't quite place, but for some reason it made her uneasy.

Nicole hesitated, walking slower and slower, until at last she came to a halt.

Ahead, she could see that something was partially blocking the path.

It was so dark that at first all she could make out was that parts of it were lighter in color than other parts, which made no sense at all.

She took a step closer. Without being aware of doing so, she slipped the backpack off and lowered it to the ground.

Another step, and the shape took form.

A body.

It was resting on its left side. The right arm was

fully extended, seemed to be reaching out, but was twisted so that the palm faced upward, the fingers curled tight into a fist.

The left arm was bent, elbow out, with the hand cushioning the head. The legs were drawn up, tucked close to the body, the way a child might lie in sleep.

But *it* was not asleep.

It was a she, and she was wearing, Nicole could see now, the familiar dark plaid skirt and white blouse that served as the school uniform. The blouse, however, wasn't white any longer.

It was soaked in what she knew had to be blood.

The face, too, was bloody; the features battered into a pulpy, misshapen mess, as though the bones had been broken and set incorrectly.

Nicole didn't want to look any more, didn't want to see anything else. Despite her resistance, her eyes were drawn to the ruined face. The girl's mouth was open, her teeth bared in a final grimace.

Nicole closed her eyes, not willing to recognize the girl, but it was already too late. She knew who it was.

"Oh, God," she whispered, and her hand flew up to cover her mouth.

Nicole swallowed hard against the nausea which threatened to overwhelm her. Her ears were ringing, and she felt dizzy, as though she might faint. She took a couple of slow, deep breaths to steady herself. When her head cleared, she opened her eyes.

The scene before her hadn't changed.

She couldn't just stand here. She had to do something. Scream? There didn't seem to be enough air in her lungs for that. And who would hear?

Run and get help, then.

No one can help her—

Nicole shook her head. Don't think about it, she told herself, determined to stay calm. Just get help.

Should she go back to the library and take a chance that Miss Shanfield would still be there? Or should she walk past the body and continue down the pathway to the school?

The wind quickened, moving through the branches of the trees, allowing her, for the first time, to see the main building. Lights shone from windows on both the ground and upper floor.

There'd be a lot of people inside.

Nicole took a step forward, moving off the pathway onto the damp grass, careful not to get too close. When she had passed the body, she turned, walking backward, not wanting to turn her back on it.

She'd only gone a few yards when her feet slipped out from under her and she landed hard on her rear end. From this angle, she could see a cascade of blond hair fanned across the grass.

Somehow, that was the worst of it.

Nicole whimpered deep in her throat.

She didn't even try to stand up.

Digging in with her heels, she pushed herself back and away, sliding on her bottom over the wet grass, only vaguely aware that her skirt had ridden up.

Only when the body was no longer in view did she get to her feet and run.

"Drink this."

Nicole accepted a mug of sugar-and milk-laced coffee, but didn't drink. It took every bit of control she had to keep from being sick to her stomach, and coffee—or anything for that matter—might prove to be her undoing.

So she sat holding the mug, both hands wrapped around it, taking comfort from the heat. Her fingers felt like ice.

Through the window in Miss Delacourt's office, she could see the flashing lights of the police cars. An ambulance had come as well, and for a brief moment she'd allowed herself to hope that she was wrong, that Melanie Whitman was still alive.

But she knew she wasn't wrong.

Nicole started to shiver again, so she put the coffee down and pulled the blanket she'd been wrapped in tighter around her. Beneath the blanket she was dressed in only her underwear; her clothes had been soaked.

One of the younger girls had been sent to get her something dry to put on. That had been ten minutes ago, and Nicole could imagine the flurry of horrified excitement in the dorm as the others— who were restricted to the second floor on Miss Delacourt's orders—crowded around to hear what few details the girl might have overheard.

Meanwhile, Miss Delacourt paced near the window, apparently deep in thought. Every few seconds she stopped and glanced speculatively in Nicole's direction, but she didn't speak.

What was there to say?

Nicole watched her. Wearing a dark gray dress which was tailored to follow the contour of her slim waist, Miss Delacourt managed to look severe and elegant at the same time. The sound of her heels on the polished wood floor echoed in the high ceilinged room.

A few salt-and-pepper wisps of hair had escaped from her chignon.

As the head mistress of Hilyer Academy, Lillian Delacourt was ultimately responsible for all of the girls. Melanie's death on campus had to be the worst thing that had ever happened—*had* to be—and yet her expression seemed composed as she stood, still for the moment, at the window. The red and blue emergency lights cast an eerie glow across her face.

Didn't she care?

"Are you all right?" Miss Delacourt asked without turning to look at her. The hint of a French accent flavored her words.

Nicole opened her mouth to answer, but it took a few seconds to find her voice. By then Miss Delacourt was facing her. "I will be," she said.

"I know what you're thinking," Miss Delacourt said.

Nicole said nothing.

"Melanie. Poor, dear Melanie. But the best

thing—the only thing—we can do for Melanie now is to protect the school that she loved so well."

Caught off guard, Nicole could only stare.

"What happened tonight is . . . tragic . . . but we mustn't allow ourselves to be drawn into sensationalism." Miss Delacourt resumed pacing. "They will try to make something tawdry of this, and *I can't let that happen.*"

They? Who were they?

"I won't let it become a—"

There was a tap at the door and Miss Fairweather, the school dorm mother, looked in. Miss Fairweather, who was eighty if she was a day, was known to take a nip now and then, and perhaps because of that, her color was high.

"Lillian," she said, in properly hushed tones, "a police officer is here to talk to Nicole."

Miss Delacourt frowned. "Can't it wait?"

"He's quite insistent."

"She's not even dressed, for heaven's sake."

The flush on Miss Fairweather's cheeks deepened. "Oh, well, it wouldn't be proper . . ."

"I want to talk to the police," Nicole said, and stood up, clutching the blanket around her. "I want them to find the person who . . . who did that to Melanie."

"Of course you do," Miss Delacourt said, "We all do. But I think you would be wise to take a few minutes to compose yourself."

Miss Fairweather looked befuddled. "Should I ask the policeman to wait?"

"I'll tell him," Miss Delacourt said, and swept from the room before Nicole could object, closing the door firmly behind her.

Miss Fairweather glanced at Nicole. "You poor child," she said. "You're shivering. I must see about getting you some warm clothes."

It wasn't the coolness of the room that was making her shiver. They were treating her like a child. "I want to talk to the police," she said again.

"There, there. Don't fret." Miss Fairweather scurried towards the door, hesitated, one hand poised above the doorknob, and looked back at Nicole. "Poor child. You really shouldn't be alone at a time like this. I know your father is out of town, but is there anyone else I can call for you, dear?"

The police, she almost said, but then had a thought. What would be the next best thing to talking to the police? "Yes, if you would. Sydney Bryant."

"Is he—"

"She," Nicole corrected. "She's a neighbor, and a very good friend of the family."

"All right. Give me her number, and I'll try to get in touch with her."

Nicole recited the phone number from memory. "Thank you, Miss Fairweather. It'll really help to have Sydney here."

"No need to thank me, dear. It's the least I can do after what you've been through."

The door clicked softly behind her.

Nicole sank back down in the chair. There was, she decided, no point in mentioning that Sydney was a private investigator.

They'd find that out soon enough.

CHAPTER ONE

Thursday, June 9th

A patrolman stood in the middle of the road, patiently signaling with a flashlight for the traffic which had slowed so the drivers could gawk, to move on. The police had closed off the entrance to Hilyer Academy with barricades, but even from the street the passersby could see the emergency lights of the squad cars and, more distant, floodlights among a grove of trees.

A crime scene.

Sydney Bryant pushed the button to lower her window, slowing the Mustang as she steered into the turning lane and braked to a stop.

"Excuse me, officer?"

He did not take his eyes off the flow of traffic. "What is it?"

"I've had a call from the school regarding one of the students, Nicole Halpern. They asked me to come down." The woman who'd phoned had been

17

vague as to why she was being summoned, but from the looks of things it couldn't be good. "What happened here?"

The cop shrugged. "I'm not at liberty to say. Talk to the man in charge."

Sydney noticed a television crew had set up in front of the polished black stone monolith which was engraved with the name of the school. They were getting ready to tape, presumably for the eleven o'clock news. It was nearly ten now.

The talent, a blonde female reporter whose range of facial expressions ran the gamut from blank to vapid to dumbstruck, fussed with her hair right up to the second that the battery-powered portable lights for the minicam flashed on.

Whatever had happened at Hilyer, it had to be pretty bad to rate a full TV crew.

The woman who'd called had assured her that Nicole was all right, but Sydney was suddenly anxious about her young neighbor's well-being. "Would you move the barricade so I can get onto the grounds?" she asked the cop.

He shrugged again, held up his hands to stop the oncoming traffic in both directions, and crossed the road. He muscled aside one section of the barrier and waved her through.

The driveway went up a slight incline, and ended in a graveled parking lot to the right of the school building. Sydney pulled into a narrow space between a patrol car and an ambulance.

The back doors of the ambulance were open, its interior lights on, revealing an impressive array of the latest in emergency medical equipment. The attendants, however, were just standing around.

And they wouldn't be unless the person they'd been called to assist and transport wasn't in need of their services.

The thought made her uneasy.

She locked the Mustang and started toward the school. The sound of police radios—garbled words and static mostly—followed her.

As she approached the building, she noticed that although the lights were off on the second floor, she could see faces at several of the windows. The ground level, by contrast, was glaringly bright, and yet there did not appear to be anyone about.

But the door opened within seconds after she knocked and an elderly, white-haired woman looked out at her with eyes that pleaded for no more surprises.

"Yes?" A frail hand fluttered at her throat.

"I'm Sydney Bryant, and I received a call—"

"Oh, yes, of course, Nicole's friend. My name is Theadora Fairweather, I'm the dorm mother here. I was the one who called you. Come in, come in."

"Is Nicole all right?"

"She says she is, although I don't know how she could be, what with all she's been through. I know *I* wouldn't be, but then a young girl would be more resilient than an old woman, I suppose." Theadora Fairweather shut and locked the door, looking visibly relieved at having done so. "I thought you were another one of those reporters

19

. . . they don't give up, you know."

"Miss Fairweather, what happened here tonight? Why are the reporters here?"

The old woman's confusion was evident. "Didn't I tell you?"

Sydney shook her head.

"Oh! I thought I had." She lowered her voice to a whisper. "A murder," she said.

The worst kind of crime scene. Sydney's instincts had been right, but she would rather have been wrong.

"One of the girls was killed this evening," Theadora Fairweather continued, "and poor, dear Nicole came upon the . . . found her along the path."

"Where is she?"

"Nicole? The police are talking to her now." She nodded in the direction of a door on the right side of the hallway a short distance from where they were standing. "They've been in there for some time."

Remarkably bright and well-adjusted at fifteen, Nicole probably didn't need anyone to hold her hand, but Sydney had seen adults become flustered and anxious when questioned by the police. She wanted to spare Nicole any further emotional trauma.

"Is anyone else in there with them?" she asked. If not, she was prepared to go in uninvited, which wouldn't exactly endear her to the police.

"Lillian . . . Miss Delacourt, that is . . . Miss Delacourt is with her."

Sydney had heard Nicole talk about Lillian Delacourt, who had taken over as headmistress last September; and who, in Nicole's estimation, was determined to turn Hilyer into some kind of finishing school, rather than focusing on academic excellence.

Nicole would not, in all likelihood, consider Lillian Delacourt an ally.

"I think Nicole would want me to be there as well," Sydney said, and took a step in that direction.

"Oh, I don't know . . . is that a good idea?"

The door in question opened just then, and a tall, slender woman came out into the hallway. The frown on her lips was quickly transformed into a careful smile when she noticed them. She drew the door closed behind her without a sound.

Somewhere, a clock began to chime the hour.

"Thea . . . I thought you'd gone upstairs," she said, but her eyes were on Sydney. "None of the girls will be able to stay awake in class in the morning if they aren't off to bed soon."

"Class? But Lillian, I thought . . . shouldn't we cancel class?"

"We mustn't allow this to disrupt the routine," Lillian Delacourt said. "If one acts as if life is normal, life will *be* normal."

Sydney doubted it. Murder had a way of changing things. "Miss Delacourt? I'm Sydney Bryant, and I'm a friend of Nicole's. I'd like to see her."

"Yes?" Her glance was measuring. "She's giving

a statement to the police . . . it would be best if you wait until they've finished.''

"Could you at least tell her I'm here?''

The smile faltered a bit. "I can't do that. The police asked me to leave them.''

Theadora Fairweather, who'd been standing by in silence, gave a little gasp. "Alone?''

Sydney caught the look that passed between the two women, but couldn't decipher it.

"Thea,'' Miss Delacourt said, "would you see to the other girls, please?''

It was, quite clearly, an order.

"Oh. Yes, of course, right away.''

Lillian Delacourt watched as Theadora hurried off, then turned again to Sydney. The smile was back.

"How did you say you know Nicole?''

She hadn't, but there was no point in saying so. "We're neighbors. And good friends.''

"And her father? You're a good friend of his also?''

Sydney inclined her head in agreement. In fact, although she'd known Ted Halpern for five years, she wasn't always sure what to make of him.

He'd raised Nicole alone after her mother died when she was only six. A brilliant X-ray crystallographer and research scientist, he'd brought his young daughter into his world, trying to fill the void in both of their lives. He took her with him on those nights and weekends when he had to work, and she'd grown up surrounded by—and at home with—the latest in technology.

As a result, Nicole was something of a whiz kid

22

with computers, a skill she had on occasion used to help Sydney on a case.

"I've tried to reach Mr. Halpern," Lillian Delacourt was saying. "I have his itinerary, but apparently he's still in transit. I've left word, of course, but as of this moment I must presume to act on his behalf as to what is in Nicole's best interests."

"Nicole might prefer—"

"Nicole is still a child," Miss Delacourt interrupted. "One does not ask a child what is best."

Sydney imagined Nicole had been relieved when the police had asked the headmistress to leave the room.

"But I think, perhaps, it would be wise if she spent the night elsewhere. I know the other girls will give her no peace . . ."

"I'd be glad to take her home with me."

Miss Delacourt made no attempt to hide her satisfaction at the offer. "Thank you. I'll notify her teachers that she's been excused from—"

The door opened again, and Sydney looked past Lillian Delacourt into the room.

Nicole sat primly on the edge of a straight-backed chair. She was wearing an oversized sweat shirt and the skirt of the school uniform, but was minus the dark blue knee socks she usually wore, and she'd tucked her bare feet beneath the chair.

Her long blond hair was damp, and it clung in untidy strands around her face. A smear of dirt marked one pale cheek. Her attention seemed focused on her hands which were folded in her lap.

Towering on either side of her were two

uniformed policemen.

"Sydney?" a familiar voice said, and she belatedly realized that it had been Lt. Mitchell Travis who'd opened the door.

At that, Nicole glanced up. "Sydney?" She got quickly to her feet, took a step, hesitated, and fell to the floor in a faint.

CHAPTER TWO

Nicole's eyes fluttered and slowly opened. She blinked twice, decisively, as though processing where she was and what she was seeing. Then a look of dismay came over her features.

"Sydney?" Her voice sounded raspy, as if it hurt her to talk.

Sydney sat on the edge of the couch beside Nicole, and took her hand. "I'm right here," she said. "Just take it easy."

"Oh, God." Her brown eyes closed again for a moment. "Please tell me I didn't faint."

Sydney brushed the hair back from Nicole's face. "It's all right, don't worry about it."

"I fainted? in front of everyone?"

"After what you've been through this evening, it's certainly understandable." More than understandable. She'd had the misfortune, over the years, to have come across a few dead bodies. The first time she'd had to fight to keep from becoming ill.

And it wasn't the kind of thing that ever got easier.

But Nicole was shaking her head. "They're already treating me as if I'm a child, or some delicate little hothouse flower who needs to be sheltered. And I have to go and faint, and prove them right. They'll never take me seriously now."

"I don't think it's as bad as that."

"Ha! I kept waiting for one of them to offer me a lollipop—"

"Are you feeling better, dear?" Lillian Delacourt had come up to stand beside them. "You gave us quite a scare, Nicole."

Nicole frowned. She was still noticeably pale, but there was determination in her eyes, and her chin tilted defiantly. "I'm sorry if I did, but now I need to talk to Sydney in private."

It was as close to rude as Sydney had ever known Nicole to be, and she wondered at the cause as she looked up to see Lillian Delacourt's reaction.

There *was* no reaction. The headmistress moved away without comment, crossing the room to where Mitch Travis was conferring with one of the patrolmen. Mitch glanced in her direction—why was it that she was always running into him?—and she turned her attention back to Nicole.

The teenager's expression had darkened.

"What is it?" Sydney asked.

A hint of a quiver played at Nicole's lower lip. "It was so terrible," she whispered.

Sydney watched her young friend work at maintaining control. She wanted to tell Nicole that it was all right to show her feelings, but something in the girl's eyes made her think that letting go at this moment might do more harm than good.

A full minute passed before Nicole was able to go on. "Whoever . . . did that to Melanie . . . he should pay. Someone has to pay."

In the ten years that she'd worked as a private investigator, Sydney had heard all kinds of people profess a desire for vengeance for all sorts of reasons—she had craved it herself once or twice—but hearing it now from Nicole was unsettling.

"He beat her," Nicole said. Tears appeared in her eyes, but she seemed oblivious to them. "He beat her so bad. Her face was . . . was *ruined*. He must have hit her, and hit her, and hit her—"

"Ssh." Sydney felt at a loss, not knowing what to say, or how to comfort her.

"She was my friend," Nicole said, and the tears spilled over. "She loaned me her notes, I'd just been studying with her and Terri, they were supposed to wait for me, finals are next week, and my notes, my books, I left them there, the sprinklers were on, and I fell, and I've got to . . . got to . . . I've got to . . ."

One of the patrolmen had been sent to get the ambulance attendant, who came into the room just as Nicole ran out of words and covered her face with her hands.

Feeling helpless, Sydney stood aside as the medic knelt by the couch.

CHAPTER THREE

"How are you doing, kid?"

Sydney glanced sideways at Lt. Mitch Travis who'd come up to stand next to her.

In his dark Italian suit and salmon-colored shirt, he didn't look at all like a cop, but he was one of the best in the San Diego Police Department. And as classy as he looked, his instincts were those of a natural-born street fighter. Those who made the mistake of underestimating him had been known to pay the price.

"I'm fine," she said. It was the same answer she always gave him, whether or not it was true.

"How is she?" he asked, indicating Nicole with a nod of his head.

The medic was checking Nicole's vital signs, talking softly to her as he pumped up the blood pressure cuff. He'd encouraged her to drink a small container of orange juice Lillian Delacourt had brought from the school kitchen, and there was now a little more color in her face.

Even so, Nicole still looked drawn.

"She'll be all right," Sydney said, more to herself than to him.

"Good. She had quite a shock . . . it was a mess out there."

Sydney turned and met his eyes. "A bad one?"

"Whoever did it made very sure that she was dead." He ran a hand through his black hair. "It was overkill, in my estimation."

"Any ideas?"

He smiled. "You would ask. But no, no ideas. It's early yet."

"What've you got so far?"

She wasn't sure he'd answer, but he did.

"The victim's name was Melanie Cerise Whitman. Age seventeen. Five foot six, maybe a hundred and ten pounds. California blond and baby blue. A pretty girl, from what I've heard, although you couldn't tell by looking at her now."

"And?"

"And what?"

"What do you think it was? A random killing? Was she just in the wrong place at the wrong time?"

"How the hell should I know?"

"I thought you might have a—"

"A theory?" His hazel eyes bore into hers. "I'm a cop; I prefer the facts."

"All right, then, what are the facts?"

He shook his head. "You can be persistent when you put your mind to it."

"That's my job."

"Ah, but you're not working, Sydney. This isn't

your case."

She didn't need to hear that. He was right, of course, but she still didn't need to hear it. "Maybe not, but Nicole is a friend of mine, and it would help to know what she's been through. She's coming home with me tonight, and she might want to talk about it."

Mitch glanced at Nicole, recognition dawning in his eyes. *"That's* where I've seen her before . . . she lives in your apartment building. It's been awhile—what is it, two years now?—but I thought she looked familiar."

It had, in fact, been three years, but even so she didn't believe for a second he hadn't placed Nicole at first sight. "Isn't forgetfulness a sign of early senility, Lieutenant?"

"I haven't forgotten you."

"Nicole said the girl was beaten," Sydney said, refusing to be sidetracked.

"You don't give up, do you?"

"Beaten with what?"

Mitch sighed. "Our old nemesis, the blunt object. Which was not found, before you ask, because I know you'll ask."

"No one saw anything?"

"Nothing to see. The place where the girl was killed is secluded, surrounded by trees. Someone standing there wouldn't be visible from any of the school buildings. Or from the street."

"But she must have cried out . . ."

"If she did, no one heard her."

"Or if they heard her . . . they didn't come running." It was a disturbing thought, and

Sydney was silent, imagining the terror of the girl's last minutes of life. "Do you know what time she was killed?"

"Just about. We know that she left the library with another girl at seven. She said she had something to do—we don't know what—and went off on her own. Nicole found her a few minutes after eight."

An hour. More than enough time to meet up with a killer.

A third patrolman had come into the room, and caught Mitch's eye. "Excuse me," he said, and touched her arm. "Don't run off . . . I want to talk to you."

Sydney watched him go.

He liked to give orders, she thought. It was too bad she didn't care to take them.

CHAPTER FOUR

Nicole was sitting with her head tilted back and her eyes closed. Her tears had dried, but her face still had the pinched look of unexpected loss.

Kneeling to one side of her, the medic whistled under his breath as he packed away the medical equipment.

A few feet away Lillian Delacourt stood; telephone to her ear, but saying nothing, apparently on hold. As she waited, her eyes flicked from the window where the emergency lights had become shrouded by the fog to Mitch, who was still consulting with his men.

An occasional word carried across the room:

Bludgeoned.

Crushed.

Bloodied.

Dead.

It wasn't, Sydney decided, the sort of thing that Nicole needed to hear right now.

The medic glanced up as she approached them.

"How is she?"

She'd spoken softly, done little more than mouth the words, but Nicole's eyes opened.

"I want to go home," Nicole said.

"Then let's go."

Nicole had slipped her bare feet into her sodden shoes which made squishing noises as they walked hurriedly down the empty hallway.

Sydney half expected someone to call after them to come back, but they made it to and out the front door without incident.

The air, heavy with moisture, felt wonderful.

Neither of them spoke. When they reached the car, Sydney unlocked the passenger door and stood aside as Nicole got in. As she closed the door, she looked around to see if anyone had noticed them.

No one had. They were too busy watching the stretcher with the victim's body being removed.

The coroner's men were attempting to roll the stretcher across the uneven terrain, but the grass apparently became entangled in its wheels. After a brief discussion, they lowered the stretcher, telescoping the runners beneath it and locking them in place, then lifted the whole apparatus off the ground.

There were perhaps thirty yards left between them and the waiting coroner's van. They crossed the distance in seconds, neither man straining under the load.

But they were big men, and the slight form beneath the blanket looked scarcely larger than a child.

Sydney stood where she was—blocking Nicole's view, if she were to look—until the stretcher had been secured in the van and the doors slammed shut. One of the men paused to light a cigarette.

The smoke from it disappeared in the swirling fog.

Traffic had thinned out considerably, owing to the late hour. The barricades were still up at the school entrance, although the patrolman who'd been tending them was nowhere in sight.

What she did see was a group of reporters.

And they saw her. Among them, towering above the rest at six foot six, was Victor Griffith.

Griffith was something of a legend in the news community. Although still in his early twenties, he had an instinct for a breaking story that defied reason. More often than not, he was the first one at the scene of fires, major accidents, and, unfortunately, homicides.

It was as if he could smell human misery, and smelling it, was fated to run it into the ground like some kind of rabid bloodhound.

A bloodhound whose relentless eyes had turned in her direction.

"Damn it." Sydney considered nosing the Mustang against the barricade to push it out of the way, but if it fell beneath the wheels, it might catch on the undercarriage of the car and do serious damage.

"Lock your door and stay in the car," she said to Nicole. She put the car in neutral, set the brake, and got out.

The reporters had started towards her, with Griffith leading the pack.

There wasn't time to be careful about it, so she grabbed the near side of the barrier and gave it a hard shove. It fell to its side and skidded noisily over the pavement before coming to rest off the driveway.

"Sydney! Wait up!"

"Right," she said under her breath. "Do I look like a masochist?"

Practically jumping back into the driver's seat, she released the brake at the same instant she depressed the clutch and shifted into first gear.

She popped the clutch. The rear ties spun and squealed as she turned right onto the three-lane road, accelerating smoothly. The big five-liter engine purred as the Mustang pulled away.

A glance in the rearview mirror showed that Griffith had followed her into the street, where he stood, hands on his hips, watching after her.

CHAPTER FIVE

Nicole remained silent during the short drive to their apartment complex, but when they pulled into the carport, Sydney could feel her begin to relax. Lillian Delacourt had been right: Nicole needed to put some distance—emotional and physical—between herself and what she'd witnessed at Hilyer Academy.

Sydney locked the car and they started toward the side entry. The parking area was lit by mercury-vapor lamps which gave the fog a greenish cast. The air was so thick with moisture it seemed to muffle the sound of their footsteps.

There was no one else about.

Nicole surprised her then by laughing. "Trouble," she said. "He's come to say hello."

Trouble was a husky black and white tomcat who belonged to the lady in 129, whose sole purpose in life seemed to be eating. He had a sweet tooth, preferring cookies to cat food, and Sydney suspected that he went door-to-door in search of

Sara Lee.

He was waiting for them just beyond the security gate, and he meowed as they approached.

Nicole squatted and reached through the wrought iron fence to stroke his nose. "What's the matter, Trouble? Are you too fat to fit through the bars?"

"Offer him a cookie," Sydney said, unlocking the gate with her key, "and he'll run through faster than you can say 'meow'."

Nicole laughed again. It did Sydney's heart good to hear it.

When they were inside the gate, Nicole picked the cat up and held him close, He tucked his head under her chin and began to purr.

"Can he come in for a little while?"

Sydney nodded. "I think I can find something in the cupboard for him."

Trouble hunkered down to eat his chocolate-chip raisin cookie. He closed his eyes as he ate, and seemed almost to smile between bites.

"Well, he likes his dinner. How about you?" Sydney asked. "Are you hungry?"

Nicole blinked. "I am, now that you mention it. I missed dinner."

Sydney had, too. She'd have to remember to call Ethan in the morning and apologize for standing him up. "I'm not much of a cook," she said, "but I think I can make something edible. Why don't you take a shower while I get things ready?"

"Okay." Nicole turned to leave, then stopped.

Her eyes met Sydney's. "Thank you for coming to the school tonight. With Dad gone . . . I don't know what I'd have done if you hadn't."

"Anytime," she said, and meant it.

Thirty minutes later they sat down to a midnight supper of scrambled eggs—which had started out to be over-easy—hash browns, thick slices of Canadian bacon, and whole wheat toast.

Nicole looked decidedly better, her skin scrubbed clean and flushed from the warmth of the shower, and dressed in Sydney's white terry cloth robe. She'd tied her towel-dried blond hair back into a ponytail, which made her look about twelve years old.

The cat hopped into Nicole's lap, curled up, and promptly fell alseep. Cats apparently didn't have sugar highs.

Nicole took a sip of milk and picked up her fork. "You know, Sydney, I have some money."

"Yes?"

"Not a lot, but I've been saving since I was a little girl."

"That's good."

"Mostly I'd save part of my allowance, and the checks I got for my birthday and Christmas. And babysitting money."

Sydney wondered where all of this was going. She didn't have to wait long to find out.

Nicole cut and speared a triangle of bacon, but didn't eat. She took a deep breath and said, "I want to hire you to find Melanie's killer."

"Oh, Nicole—"

"I know you can do it. I know you can."

"Honey, it's not as simple as whether or not I could do it—and I'm not as sure as you are that I could. Murder is police business, and they don't take kindly to anyone getting in their way."

"But they *won't* find him. All of the murders that you hear about on the news . . . how many times do they find the guy?"

"It's not from lack of trying. And they do catch some of them."

"Maybe they do, but they haven't been able to catch that guy who's been killing all those women and dumping the bodies off the side of the road." Her expression darkened. "I mean, you'd think if he's sick enough to keep on doing it, he couldn't be that smart. That sooner or later, the cops would catch him at it, or somebody would come along and see him."

"Sooner or later, somebody will," Sydney said, although she wasn't quite sure she believed it.

That particular series of murders had been going on for years. Recently there'd been speculation in the press that the infamous Green River killer from Washington state had traveled south to San Diego.

If so, the man had been getting away with murder for a very long time.

"And they're always saying the police department is understaffed, that there aren't enough policemen to patrol the streets—"

"Nicole, this is homicide. Investigating your friend's death will be a top priority."

"But what does that *mean?*" She finally ate the

piece of bacon and began to poke at her eggs with the fork.

Sydney was silent for a moment. What it probably didn't mean was the kind of single-minded dedication that Nicole wanted. And not because they weren't anxious to solve the crime. The realities of police work quite simply would not allow the investigating officers to concentrate solely on the girl's murder.

Other cases would demand attention. Ongoings might be put aside for a day or two, but inevitably they would return to the forefront. Court appearances and days off would also whittle away at the time police spent on Melanie's case.

And the more time that passed, the less likely the murder would be solved.

Still, the police had resources she couldn't hope to match. She was working a surveillance on a worker's compensation case, and running a couple of skip traces—finding people who'd skipped out on their bills—as well. None of which was as critical as a murder, but such cases were the bread-and-butter of a private investigator's job.

"Please," Nicole said. "I'm not saying that Melanie was my closest friend—she was a senior and I'm only a sophomore—but we were studying together just a few minutes before she was . . . was killed. She lent me her lab workbook. And I was the one who found her . . ." Her voice trailed off to a whisper.

"That doesn't make you responsible," Sydney said gently. "I understand how you feel—"

Nicole's hands had clenched into fists. "Why do people always say that? No one understands.

Unless they've been through it, how could they?"

Sydney inclined her head in agreement. She was willing to concede the point.

"Maybe it's not my responsibility," Nicole continued, "but I can't just go on with my life and pretend it never happened."

"What about Melanie's parents? This is really their concern."

"But they're *not* concerned. Melanie told me once that she hadn't even seen her father since she started at Hilyer. She never knew her mother, I guess. They weren't married, but her father had the money so he took her to live with him. Only she didn't, because he was never around."

"Then the school—"

Nicole shook her head. "Miss Delacourt cares more about the fact that I got grass stains on my underwear—nice girls don't, you know—than that Melanie is dead."

"Even if that's true—"

"Help me, Sydney. Please."

She sighed. If she took the case, she'd have to keep a low profile to keep from ruffling the police department's feathers. That might prove difficult, since she'd no doubt need to talk to the same people they would interview.

Still, if she played it right . . .

As far as her own work went, the weekend was coming up and the skip traces, at least, could easily be put off until Monday. Or later?

"All right," she said at last. "I'll see what I can do."

CHAPTER SIX

Friday, June 10th

The tickle of cat whiskers woke her, and Sydney opened her eyes to find Trouble standing on her pillow gazing into her face.

The pale light of early morning streamed through the venetian blinds. A glance at the clock confirmed that it was not yet six a.m.

"What is it, Trouble?" She rubbed a silky ear. "Have a breakfast date?"

His purr rasped in his throat, uneven at first but finally catching hold into an impressive rumble. He began to knead and dig at the pillow, extending and retracting his claws.

It would, she thought, be nice to spend the day curled up in bed—or in this case, the sofabed—with nothing more to do than listen to a cat's purr. There was something about the sound that invited inertia.

Her eyelids were almost closed again when the

telephone rang.

"What now?" she said to him, reaching for the phone. "Did you leave a wake-up call?"

The cat meowed. Tail straight in the air, he jumped down and walked off.

"Hello?"

"Sydney? This is Ted Halpern."

All at once she was fully awake. She sat up and with one hand brushed her hair out of her face. "Ted. I assume you've heard."

"I've heard. I'd have called last night, but it was late when I got in." The line crackled with static. "How is Nicole? How is she taking it?"

They weren't easy questions to answer, and she took a few moments before she replied. "You know Nicole. One minute you'd swear she had a good forty years of hard living behind her, and the next you expect to see her wearing pigtails and playing hopscotch."

Ted laughed. "She can be that way, all right. Sometimes I'm not sure which of us is the parent."

Sydney heard the homesickness in his voice. "I think she's going to be fine. It may take awhile, but she's going to get through this."

"Should I come home? I can be on a plane in a few hours."

"I don't know. I'm sure Nicole would like to have you home with her, but there's nothing to be done. And the worst is over, at least for now." Testifying in court, if it ever came to that, might prove to be another kind of hell. "She's given a statement to the police," Sydney continued. "And

44

she's resilient."

"Yes, I suppose." He paused, and when he spoke again he sounded as though the words were hard to say. "When I saw the message, to call the school, I thought . . . I thought I'd lost her."

Sydney felt a flash of anger at that. Hadn't Lillian Delacourt the sense to leave a message which wouldn't be misinterpreted?

"My hands," he said, "were shaking so badly, I had to ask the clerk to dial the phone."

"My God, Ted." She closed her eyes.

"I tried to brace myself while the phone was ringing, for whatever was coming, but there's no bracing yourself for the loss of a child."

She thought of Melanie Whitman and what Nicole had told her last night. Was the girl's father grieving? Did he even know his daughter was dead?

"And when I finally understood what she was saying, what I was hearing, I felt such an overwhelming sense of relief . . . but then I realized that it could have been Nicole . . . who was murdered."

Sydney wanted to deny it could happen, but she knew as well as he did that the most frightening thing about death was how random it could be.

Neither of them spoke for a minute.

"Do you want me to wake her?" she asked finally.

"If you would."

She'd started to put the receiver down when she heard him call her name. She returned the phone to her ear. "Yes?"

"Take care of her for me?"

"I will."

Nicole stayed on the phone with her father for a long time. Sydney put the cat out—he headed straight for his own home where no doubt he had a breakfast Danish waiting—and then made up the sofabed.

She dressed in jeans and an embroidered peasant blouse she'd picked up in Tijuana, and ran a brush through her ash blond hair. Her reflection in the mirror looked the way it always did when she'd had too little sleep, so she decided not to look.

She was in the kitchen when the murmur of Nicole's voice stopped. A moment later Nicole came in, wrapped in the terry cloth robe, a faint smile on her face.

"Good morning," Sydney said. "Are you hungry?"

"No, thanks." Nicole patted her tummy. "I think I'm still full from last night."

That was no surprise. After they'd finished talking—and although the food had grown cold—Nicole had cleaned her plate. She'd put slices of bacon on a piece of toast, covered that with eggs and a mound of hash browns, topped it with a second slice of toast, squashed the whole thing flat, and ate it all.

For her own part, Sydney found it hard to look at food until after ten or so. She popped the tab on an ice-cold can of Pepsi and took a swallow, savoring the way it tingled her throat.

"So. What do you want to do today?"

Nicole gave her a perplexed look. "What do you mean? I've got to go to school."

"You've been excused from school."

"Excused?"

"Miss Delacourt said she'd tell your teachers not to expect you in class."

"I *have* to go to school. Finals start on Monday, and there'll be review sessions in all of my classes today. I have to go."

Sydney knew that Nicole carried an A average. There was little chance she'd fail any subject if she missed a day, review sessions or not. And being on campus might be difficult for her. If she looked out a window and saw the place where she'd found her friend's body, that alone could be enough to upset the delicate emotional equilibrium she'd forged for herself.

The other girls could hardly be expected to contain their curiosity. There would be tears and whispers and not-so-carefully veiled glances.

The police were bound to be around as well.

On the other hand, if Nicole could concentrate on her studies—and Nicole could do it if anyone could—it might be the best thing for her, to keep her mind off what had happened.

"All right," Sydney said. "If that's what you want."

"It is."

While Nicole went down to the Halpern apartment to get a fresh uniform to wear, Sydney called her answering service to pick up her messages.

Daphne, the night operator and the best of the bunch, was still on duty.

"I thought you'd fallen off the face of the earth," Daphne said. "It's not like you not to call in. Isn't your pager working?"

"I turned it off."

"Oh . . . a romantic interlude?"

Sydney smiled. "No, nothing like that."

"More's the pity, dear. Well, you got a lot of calls. Ethan Ross called twice, no, make that three times. That man has a great voice."

"I know."

"And your mother called."

"From New York?" She and Ethan's mother—friends and neighbors since they were young brides after the Second World War—had gone to New York for a week of shopping and sightseeing, but especially to attend a performance of *Les Misérables*.

"Yes. She sends her love and said to tell you she'd call back this weekend. And she wants you not to work so hard."

That sounded like her mother, all right. "Anything else?"

"A Lieutenant Travis wants you to call him first thing this morning, and he said it was urgent."

"Right."

"And last, but not least, I had a very strange call from a Mr. Griffith."

Victor. "Did he leave a message?"

"I suppose you could call it that. He said, and I quote, 'It's not nice to ignore your friends.'"

"Hmm."

"He also said he'd be seeing you later."

"I can hardly wait."

"He left a number if you want it."

"No, no. I have Mr. Griffith's number."

"Well, then, that's the lot."

"Thanks. I think."

Daphne chuckled. "I'd call Mr. Ross if I were you. Whoops, I gotta go. I've got a line about to ring off the board."

Sydney hung up the phone. It was too early to call Mitch and she had no intention of calling Griffith. As for Ethan . . .

The front door opened and Nicole came in, her school clothes folded over her arm. There was, Sydney noticed, a marked lessening of tension in her young face. Had those few minutes in her own apartment brought about the change?

If so, Dorothy in *The Wizard of Oz* was right: there was no place like home.

One of the cars ahead of them was all over the road, drifting in and out of the lane.

Sydney wondered idly if the driver was one of those people who as a child couldn't—or refused to—color within the lines.

More likely, he or she was drunk.

She kept her distance, and glanced sideways at Nicole, who was gazing silently out the window. What was she thinking, Sydney wondered.

And then they were at the school, turning past the black monolith, and up toward the main building.

CHAPTER SEVEN

By the light of day, Hilyer Academy was an impressive sight.

Built on a slight rise in the land, the school proper was housed in a stately mansion that would not have been out of place in the antebellum South. Adding to that impression were the magnificent magnolia trees on either side of the entrance.

Beyond were lush, green, gently sloping hills. Thick trees shaded sections of the cut-stone pathways which branched to both the right and left of the main building.

Although the road was nearby, it was surprisingly quiet on the campus. The only sounds were those of the wind rustling through the trees, and the plaintive cooing of a mourning dove.

It would be hard to find a more unlikely place for a murder.

Sydney glanced automatically toward the spot where the flood lights had been. The yellow police line tapes were still in place, warning off the curious.

Nicole kept her eyes averted.

There were two girls in the front hall near the door to Lillian Delacourt's office. When they saw Nicole they nudged each other, and began to whisper.

Nicole lifted her chin. "Hi Steffi, Becky."

The taller of the two smiled a bit hesitantly. "Nicole. Are you ready for the algebra final?"

"I wish."

The second girl made a face. "If *you're* not ready, nobody is. And if I don't pass, I'll be grounded 'til I'm eighty."

"You mean eighteen," her friend corrected.

"No, I mean eighty. You don't know my parents."

The three of them laughed, Nicole a little uncertainly.

"Girls!" someone called. "Please!"

Theadora Fairweather came bustling around a corner, a scowl on her face. "Show a little consideration. There are others trying to . . . trying to . . ."

Her voice trailed off. Apparently seeing Nicole had interrupted her train of thought.

"Trying to study," Nicole offered.

"Study? Why, yes. They are."

Sydney took a step forward. "Miss Fairweather, as you can see, Nicole has decided to come to school today after all."

"Yes, I can . . . oh, Nicole, I have something of yours, just wait a minute and I'll get it for you, dear." She hurried off, muttering to herself.

Steffi and Becky waited until she'd turned the corner and then shared a conspiratorial look with Nicole, all of them raising their eyebrows dramatically.

"Eighty," Becky said.

Sydney expected them to break into giggles, but at that moment the dorm mother returned lugging a dangerously overstuffed Jansport backpack.

"A nice policeman brought this by."

Nicole gave a sigh of relief. "Thank goodness, my notes—"

"Nicole?"

The door to Lillian Delacourt's office had opened soundlessly, and the headmistress stepped into the hall. In her high-necked white blouse and straight black skirt, her hair worn in a chignon, she looked the part.

Her cool glance moved slowly from Nicole to Sydney, and then back again. The others she ignored.

"I didn't expect you in school today, Nicole."

The easy camaraderie of seconds before was gone. Steffi opened the book she was carrying and flipped through the pages, as though searching for something. Becky examined her nails, frowning.

Nicole, however, met Lillian Delacourt's eyes. "I'm here," she said.

"Yes, so I see." Her gaze returned to Sydney. "Miss Bryant . . ."

"Miss Delacourt?"

"I wonder if I might have a word with you?"

"Of course."

"You girls had better run along to class," the headmistress said, still not looking at them. "Thea . . . would you please see to it that we're not disturbed?"

Theadora Fairweather started, as if she were about to jump out of her skin, but she nodded and began to make little shooing motions at the girls.

Nicole hesitated. "Sydney . . ."

"Don't worry," Sydney said under her breath. "Go on to class. Remember what we talked about . . ."

Sydney sat in the chair indicated and waited while Lillian Delacourt sat down, scribbled a note in a file, closed it, and centered it on her desk.

"I understand," she said, leaning forward, "that you're a private detective."

"Yes."

"Really. It must be a fascinating line of work."

"It has its moments."

"I'm sure it does. The officer who informed me of your occupation spoke quite highly of you."

Sydney allowed herself a smile. "That's always nice to hear."

"Isn't it?" Her manicured fingers picked up a business card which had been tucked beneath the bottom left corner of the desk blotter. "Mitchell Travis. Lieutenant Travis, to afford him the respect due his rank. He said you were skilled enough to be with the police."

"I'll have to thank him for that the next time I see him."

"Nicole never mentioned that you were a detective."

"Should she have?"

"Perhaps not. But I wonder, Miss Bryant, why you did not?"

"I wasn't here in my capacity as a private investigator. I was here as Nicole's friend."

"And this morning?"

Sydney merely smiled.

Lillian Delacourt ran her thumbnail absently along the edge of Mitch's business card. "How is Nicole this morning?" she asked.

That, Sydney thought, should have been her first question. "Quite well. She didn't want to miss the review sessions in her classes."

"Hmm. She's an excellent student, very conscientious, although she can be stubborn at times."

"At times," Sydney agreed. "But only about things that matter."

The woman's icy eyes regarded her. "Still, she is a child—"

"Kids grow up faster these days."

"I'm not convinced of that. If anything, I think it's the other way around. If, in fact, they grow up in an emotional sense at all, it's not until they are forced to do so. And most are not. What we have in this country is an abundance of very childish adults and their pseudo-sophisticated children."

"It's an interesting theory."

"It's more than that, I can assure you. But—" she shook her head "—that is not what I wanted to talk to you about."

Sydney waited for her to go on.

"A horrible thing has happened. A young girl's life has been cut short. It is a tragic, tragic incident. I have not yet fully comprehended that Melanie . . . is dead." She paused, and laced her fingers together in front of her. "Melanie has . . . had attended Hilyer since she was thirteen. Hilyer was her home for the last four years. I have only been with the school since September, but I feel I can speak for the staff and students when I say it's as if we've lost a member of our family."

They were the right words, but Sydney did not sense that they were deeply felt.

"There is nothing I or anyone can do to bring Melanie back, however hard we might wish it. I am responsible for the well-being of the rest of the girls, and to that end, I have decided the best thing for all concerned is to put it behind us."

"That may not be easy."

"Oh, I know there's nothing I can do about the police. They will conduct their investigation regardless of any objections I might raise. As they should. And the girls will no doubt need time to get over it, although I've taken some steps to accelerate that process. But what I can do is keep Melanie's death from becoming a media event."

Sydney arched her eyebrows. "How do you propose to do that?"

"Obviously, my first step will be to close the campus. I've contracted with a security company to provide twenty-four hour guard service. The reporters will not be allowed on the grounds."

"You'd be surprised at how resourceful a reporter after a story can be," she said, thinking of Victor Griffith.

"I've been assured that the campus will be secure."

Sydney wasn't going to argue.

"Then," Lillian Delacourt continued, "I've enlisted the cooperation of my staff. They will not be giving any statements to the press."

"I see."

"And, finally, the school's attorney has requested the police department not to release any further information regarding Melanie's death, including her name."

Sydney blinked, surprised. "They agreed?"

"For now at least. I've been unable to reach her father, nor has anyone been able to determine her mother's whereabouts. Since Melanie was a minor and her family has not been notified . . . they really had no choice."

There was no mistaking the satisfaction in the woman's eyes. "If everything is under control, why did you want to talk to me?"

"Ah. Because Nicole is at the heart of it."

"And?"

"I had a call from Mr. Halpern this morning. He'd indicated when we talked last night he might be coming home, but I gather he is heading several committees and is presenting a paper of some importance. So he instructed me that Nicole was to be given over to your care. And I must enlist your assistance."

Sydney wasn't sure what was coming, but something surely was.

"I'd planned to call you, but since you're here . . . I think it best if Nicole not attend school for the rest of the term."

"What?"

"I don't pretend to know your circumstances, but I have been authorized to pay you whatever your daily rate is for the next ten days to keep Nicole in your care, and out of sight."

"That's—"

"Since she's already here this morning, she can stay for the review sessions, of course. But after today, it would be best—for her as well—if she wasn't on campus. Classes are over for the year, and she'll be allowed to take her finals later, at her convenience."

"Miss Delacourt—"

"Please—" she held up a hand "—let me finish. I have a check for you, as a retainer." She opened the center desk drawer, extracted a sealed envelope, and held it out. "If it's not enough—"

"I can't accept your check."

A tiny furrow appeared between her eyebrows. "And why not?"

"I already have a client who hired me to conduct an investigation into what happened here at Hilyer."

The furrow deepened. "Who might that be?"

"I can't tell you; my client prefers I keep that information confidential." Sydney stood up. "Now, if you'll excuse me . . ."

CHAPTER EIGHT

Theadora Fairweather was hovering about in the hall when Sydney left Lillian Delacourt's office. She offered Sydney a tentative smile.

But the smile quickly faded, and Sydney sensed that the headmistress had followed her. A glance over her shoulder confirmed it.

The woman stood in the doorway. "You realize, of course, that Melanie's school records are confidential as well, according to the state education code," Miss Delacourt said. "I am not requird to, nor will I, divulge any details of her enrollment here."

"Whatever," Sydney said, and with a nod to Theadora she departed.

With Nicole busy in class, Sydney decided to head for her office in University City. There were calls she had to make, and paperwork she needed to finish before starting up this investigation.

As she drove she made a mental list of sources to tap for information on Melanie Whitman; because, although it was entirely possible her death had indeed been random, most murder victims were acquainted with their killers. The logical place to start was with the victim's family and friends.

Unfortunately, the people she wanted to interview first—Melanie's teachers and classmates, including Terri Allison, who as far as anyone knew had been the last person to see Melanie alive—would not be available until after three.

If even then. Lillian Delacourt had made it clear she should not expect a great deal of cooperation from the Hilyer staff.

That didn't particularly worry her. One of the fascinating things about being an investigator was the many ways there were of getting information when the most obvious sources were not available.

But . . . the logical place to start was with Melanie's background. Knowing more about Melanie would help her ask the right questions.

Background usually equals family. After a great deal of thought, Nicole had managed to recall the father's name: Albert Locke Whitman.

Sydney recognized the name and even the face that went with it. A.L. Whitman's photograph showed up sporadically in society columns—reading them was her secret passion—usually with a much younger woman on his arm. He met the minimum basic requirements for social fame: he was tall and blond, reasonably attractive, had the requisite tan, was fashionably slim, and, most importantly, was stinking rich.

Inherited money, she thought. As with others who'd inherited their wealth, he didn't hesitate to spend—or squander?—the family fortune. It was unlikely he'd ever held a job.

He was one of that rare breed who didn't just fly, but 'jetted.'

What she recalled most from his photographs, though, was that the corners of his mouth seemed to turn down even when he smiled. His eyes were those of a man who'd seen too much, done too much, *had* too much, and still wasn't happy.

It shouldn't be difficult to trace someone of his standing and notoriety. His comings and goings would be duly noted by those who were paid to chronicle the odysseys of the rich.

The mother was another story.

Nicole couldn't remember Melanie ever calling her mother by name. That would make tracking her considerably more difficult, if not impossible. Since Melanie's parents had never married, there wouldn't have been a marriage license issued, a betrothal announced, or for that matter, a divorce petition filed.

And as far as the country had come since its puritanical days, illegitimate births still weren't a topic for society news.

Sydney couldn't assume that the mother was from San Diego, or California, or even the United States. Given A.L. Whitman's lifestyle, Melanie's mother might be of any nationality. And she very well could have chosen to have her child on her own home ground.

So where to look to find her? And, considering the woman apparently had no contact with Melanie, was it even necessary to find her?

No use in making things more difficult than they already were. Begin with the father.

A call to her contact at the Department of Motor Vehicles would give her the man's date of birth and current address—or Melanie's, since at seventeen, she'd been old enough to drive—and work from there.

It was a place to start.

Her office was located on the second floor of a U-shaped building which also was home to a printing shop, Luigi's Delicatessen, a liquor store, a video rental center, an insurance office, and a clothing store specializing in "hard to fit" sizes.

When busines at Bryant Investigations was slow, she sometimes thought she should bring in a TV and her VCR. She could get one of Luigi's huge turkey, bacon and avocado sandwiches; rent a couple of video tapes, and spend all day watching movies.

In no time at all, she'd be a customer at the "hard to fit" store.

The classic solution for an underworked private eye was to hit the bottle—thereby utilizing the downstairs liquor store—but alcohol went straight to her head. She couldn't even drink white wine. Or rather, shouldn't.

Luckily, business had been fairly steady of late, due in part to the publicity she'd received last

February when she'd been hired to search for the missing wife of a prominent La Jolla surgeon.

She'd found the missing wife, but there'd been no happily-ever-after ending. The last she'd heard, the surgeon was on a month-long honeymoon cruise with his new wife, a beautiful British-born Chinese nurse who was every bit as self-absorbed as he was.

She sighed and pulled into a parking place.

It was time to get to work.

The mail had come early and she collected it from the floor. One of her statements had come back with the red-stamped notation that the addressee had moved and left no forwarding address.

"Great." Although she did skip traces routinely, it was usually for a client. She hated tracing her own deadbeats; having to do so reminded her that she wasn't always such a good judge of people.

On the plus side, she'd finally gotten the check for a corporate espionage case she'd worked three months back, and her MasterCard bill wasn't too high.

There was also a direct-mail envelope, bulging with coupons for things she never needed and services she couldn't imagine wanting. Twenty dollars off a psychic reading. A free spinal exam. Ten percent off leg waxing. Or the real savings: a fifty dollar discount on a dental appliance used for losing weight.

She had better uses for her money.

Then again, there were those sandwiches of Luigi's . . . she ran a critical hand over her fanny. Was she gaining weight?

The door to the office opened behind her.

"I'll be glad to do that for you if you want," a familiar voice said.

Sydney groaned and turned to face the door. "Victor," she said. "What a surprise."

"You mean, 'what a pleasant surprise,' don't you?"

CHAPTER NINE

As always when she saw Victor Griffith at close quarters, she was startled by how much he resembled the character of Ichabod Crane. He wore his thinning brown hair in a Prince Valient cut, which only accentuated the abnormal length of his neck and the unfortunate prominence of his Adam's apple.

"Victor," she said.

He laughed and crossed to the chair in front of her desk where he sat down, stretching out his long legs. "If you need a physical trainer, somebody to whip you into shape, I'm your man."

"I can see that." Although tall and gangly, there was, beneath his ill-fitting clothes, the suggestion of softness.

He caught her look. "Oh, I don't mean that *I'm* in shape . . . the only exercise I get is jumping to conclusions. But I'm willing to help you work up a sweat, and I've got an eye for the feminine form."

"I'll keep it in mind," she said dryly. "So what

do you want?"

"Guess."

"I'm afraid I can't help you. I don't know any more than you do."

"Come on, Sydney, don't give me that. You were there at the school and you left with one of the students."

"That doesn't mean—"

"It means," he interrupted, "that you at least know the murdered girl's name."

"And you don't?"

He shook his head. "The cops are refusing to release her name. The old name-withheld-pending-notification-of-relatives bit. And so far, I haven't been able to sniff it out."

"What's wrong with waiting? No other reporter's going to hear it before you do."

"Hey! I am not just your average reporter. I am a media star."

"Your modesty is refreshing."

"Damn right. So when I get something tasty, with a shot at the front page, I like to go the distance. Do the background story. Dig up whatever's there is to dig up. Give it a little more than the usual who-what-where-when-why. Make it hard for the editor to blue pencil my copy."

"What's that have to do with me?"

"I'm missing the who. Without the who, it's no story. Maybe a paragraph, and I don't do paragraphs. All I've got so far is that she was seventeen, a student at got-bucks Hilyer Academy, and somebody beat the tar out of her last night."

Sydney frowned. "Show a little respect, will you?"

"I don't have *time* for respect." He pulled at the sleeves of his jacket in a futile attempt to make them cover his bony wrists. "But I'll make a deal with you. You give me her name and I'll send my respects . . . a dozen roses to the funeral."

"You can be the most aggravating—"

"—annoying, bothersome, vexatious, irritating asshole. I know the drill, and I've got a thesaurus, so I know all the words."

She regarded him. "Not all of them."

"But we've gotten off the subject. I need the girl's name. Then I can burrow into the library at the paper like a maggot in rotting flesh."

One of Griffith's less endearing qualities was his fondness for grossing people out. She kept her expression blank, unwilling to play his game. "Sorry. You'll have to wait for the police to release it, because I have nothing to say."

"Tsk, tsk, Sydney."

"Now I have work to do, so if you don't mind?"

He rose awkwardly to his feet. "I never mind, you should know that, but don't blame me if some other vixen with a more amiable attitude steals my heart away—petty theft, though that might be— because you wouldn't be a good little private dick and help me out."

"Goodbye, Victor. Don't forget to shut the door when you leave."

"I'll leave," he said, "but I won't go away."

CHAPTER TEN

Sydney called the DMV, but as usual the line was busy. It took a dozen tries before she got through, and even then she had to listen to a recorded message which advised her to make an appointment. In all the times she'd been to the DMV office, only once had she seen anyone there by appointment. The poor soul had forgotten to bring some vital piece of paper and had been sent away.

That was how they treated appointment holders. It was hardly an incentive to comply.

Eventually, an operator came on the line and her call was put through.

"Barbara," she said when she heard her friend's voice. "It's Sydney."

"Sydney, as I live and breathe. Where've you been? I haven't heard from you in ages."

She smiled. On Monday she'd asked for and gotten license information on five individuals pertaining to the skip traces. "Yes, well, time does fly. I have some names for you, if you're not too busy."

"Me busy? Never. Don't you know they train us how to avoid work? All I do is shuffle papers, staple them, and put them on a stack. What happens to them after that, I haven't a clue. Hey, maybe I could hire you to find out . . . but why should I care?"

Sydney laughed. "That must be the reason they made you supervisor."

"Absolutely. So give me the names. I don't want to be late for my coffee break."

"Albert Locke—that's Locke with an e—Whitman. And Melanie Cerise Whitman."

"Whitman," Barbara said, "got it. Anything else?"

"That'll do it for now."

"All right. I'll call you back after I run these. Twenty minutes?"

"Thanks, Barbara," she said, and hung up.

Next she tried calling Mitch Travis, and was informed that he was "in the field." She declined to leave a message; even three years after their affair had ended there was still talk about them. She wasn't going to add fuel to the fire by leaving her name.

She then dialed Ethan's law office.

Ethan's secretary, the ever-efficient Valentine Lund, informed her in crisp tones that Ethan was in court, probably for the entire day.

"When you talk to him, would you tell him I'm sorry I didn't make it for dinner last night?"

"Oh?"

How, Sydney wondered, did the woman manage to pack such arch disapproval into a one syllable word? "I'll be at my office until noon if he happens to check in with you during a recess."

"At your office. I'll tell him."

"Thank you," she said, but Valentine had already hung up.

She dropped the receiver into the cradle and contemplated the rest of the morning. Wait for Barbara to call. Wait for Ethan to call. Try another time or two to reach Mitch.

There was nothing else to do except paperwork.

Sydney opened the file on the workmen's compensation case, reviewing her notes to date.

The subject, a twenty-seven year old woman who'd been employed as a grocery clerk at a major supermarket, was claiming total disability for a back injury. She'd been injured after she'd slipped in a puddle of melted Frusen Gläcè.

The ice cream was on the floor because a customer had been "grazing"—eating from the packages in her cart—while she shopped. The plastic spoon she'd used to sample her deli potato salad and yogurt had broken when she'd tried to scoop out the hard frozen desert.

The wedge of ice cream flew off, landing on the floor. The customer made no attempt to clean it up, nor had she alerted store personnel.

Along came the grocery clerk.

The insurance company which had hired Sydney did not deny the accident had taken place, or that the clerk was injured, but as a rule they were suspicious of back injury claims. And total disability claims were naturally even more suspect.

The orthopaedic surgeon treating the clerk had been reluctant to either substantiate or refute his patient's claims. Pain wouldn't show up on X-rays, range of motion could be consciously limited, and the prospect of unearned money might tempt anyone to fake it. For his part, the doctor was only showing the caution inherent in practicing medicine in these litigious days.

Angered at what she considered the insurance company's foot dragging, the clerk had threatened to sue everyone involved. The store, she contended, was responsible for the customer's negligence, since they had willfully established that grazing was acceptable behavior by having free sample tables where all kinds of foods were handed out to people who then roamed the aisles while eating.

She had been hired to watch the clerk. If the woman was indeed faking, Sydney would document—through photographs and videotape later, if warranted—the proof. Could she reach her arms over her head? Could she bend down and pick up a newspaper? Was she able to walk fast, and presumably free of pain?

It was amazing that sometimes the same people who moaned and winced with every step under their doctor's assessing eye would, at home, let their guard down and go out to mow the lawn; wash the car; or, in one case she'd worked, go off to their regular Thursday night bowling game.

This case hadn't been that cut-and-dried. For the week that Sydney'd been watching, the clerk had been essentially housebound the entire time. When she *did* come out, she moved stiffly.

Sydney rather thought the insurance company might have to pay on this one.

She had almost finished typing her report when the phone rang.

"What happened to you?"

"Ethan." She changed the phone from her left hand to her right. "Listen, I'm sorry about last night. I had an urgent call and when I tried to reach you to cancel, you'd already left."

"I thought it had to be something like that. You'll be glad to know I ordered your favorite dinner—"

"Yakitori?"

"Right. It was very, very good."

Sydney groaned, remembering cold scrambled eggs. "You had to tell me."

"I believe in full disclosure," he laughed.

"You have a mean streak, counselor."

"So what was it that kept you last night?"

She told him, briefly, of the death of Melanie Whitman and of Nicole's connection with the case.

Ethan, who'd been a policeman for seven years before quitting to go to law school, listened without interrupting. When she had finished, he said, "I'd watch my step if I were you, Sydney. The investigating officer is not going to like you nosing around."

"Like it or not, I'm in this, and I'm going to do my damnedest to come up with some answers. If nothing else, I want to know why Lillian Delacourt is so anxious to keep this thing quiet."

"Well, if they bust you for interfering with an officer in performance of his duties, give me a call and I'll bail you out."

"I'll hold you to that."

"I'd better get back to court before the judge cites me for contempt. Take care of yourself."

Sydney smiled and hung up the phone which immediately began to ring.

"Bryant Investigations."

"Syd, this is Barbara. I've got the goods."

She grabbed a pencil and pad. "Shoot."

"All right. First, Whitman, Albert Locke. Address as of September 2nd, 1981 is 465 Beverly Drive, La Jolla. Male, six foot one, a hundred and sixty. Blond and gray. Class one license, status valid. Am I going too fast?"

"No, I've got it. Go on."

"No departmental actions, no convictions, no failure to appear, and no accidents."

Sydney wondered if Whitman employed a chauffeur to do his driving.

"Now, for Whitman, Melanie Cerise. Same address. Five foot six, a hundred and two. Blond and blue. Class one license, status valid. She's clean with us on all four counts. And that's it."

"Registered vehicles?"

"Oh, right. Just one, a 1987 Chevrolet IROC,

registered to her at that address. Registration is current, but expires in September."

It *would* expire in September, Sydney thought as she thanked Barbara and hung up. Where was the car? As far as she knew, the Hilyer students weren't allowed to have cars in residence.

At the house on Beverly, then.

CHAPTER ELEVEN

The house on Beverly was something to behold. It sat at the end of a cul-de-sac in one of the more exclusive neighborhoods in La Jolla.

Its three levels were in steps, and seemed almost to climb up the hillside behind it.

As usual for property with an ocean view, the house appeared to be built of glass. The morning overcast, typical of June, hadn't quite cleared yet; but rays of sunshine had broken through, and the golden light was reflected in the windows.

Whoever had designed the Whitman house had been an optimist, she thought, considering an earthquake fault ran inland from where it originated under the ocean floor and cut through the town. But, if someone could afford a place like this, they could afford to rebuild if it came to that.

Sydney swung around the cul-de-sac and parked on the street facing away from the house. She was just about to open the door and get out, when she saw a police car approach and pull into the

Whitman driveway.

She stayed put, watching in her sideview mirror as a uniformed officer went up to the house and rang the bell. As he waited, he hooked his thumbs in his belt and glanced toward the street.

She sunk a little lower in the seat. Luckily, the Mustang seats were high-backed, and she doubted he could see her.

The door opened and a woman dressed in funereal black stepped out. She listened, nodding, as the policeman spoke. With a wave of her hand, she ushered him inside. The door closed.

Sydney's attention was caught by a flurry of movement across the road. A man had apparently drawn back a drape to look out at her. Then the drape fell back into place, the door flew open, and he was coming in her direction.

Something about his gleeful expression told her this wasn't a homeowner concerned that she was loitering on his street.

He winked at her when he'd reached midpoint in the road. "How are ya?" he asked.

He was a small man, perhaps her height at five foot four, and had that bantam rooster kind of slimness suggesting barely restrained energy. A fringe of dark hair ringed his bald head, but he had wisely decided against letting it grow and plastering the strands across his pate. Blue eyes sparkled from beneath bristly brows.

Dressed in pink and red plaid shorts, a lavender shirt, peppermint-striped knee socks and sandals, he was anything but unobtrusive. The Russians

78

could probably pick him out on their satellite photos.

"Hello," she said.

"I saw you looking at the party boy's place," he said. He bent over, rested his arms on the car door and peered in at her. "I have to say, you don't look like one of his sweeties . . ."

"I'm not—"

"Of course, he could have all of a sudden got some taste." He smiled, showing movie star teeth. "My name's Orenthal O'Shea. My friends call me Oh-oh."

"Mr. O'Shea." She extended her hand. "I'm Sydney Bryant."

"Polite, too," he said, shaking it. "That settles it, you're definitely not one of his. Those girlies with their drop-dead looks don't have a cordial bone in their skinny little bodies. He's welcome to them, if you ask me."

Sydney hadn't, but she smiled. Over the years, she'd learned a lot by listening to the neighbors.

"So," he said, "if you're not an ice maiden, what are you doing here?"

She glanced in the sideview mirror; there was no sign of the cop. "I was hoping to talk to the housekeeper about Melanie Whitman."

"Melly? You know Melly?"

Sydney hesitated. She'd assumed that word of Melanie's death would have circulated through the neighborhood, but it was clear that Mr. O'Shea wasn't aware of what had happened to the girl.

He caught her uncertainty. "What is it?" The

bluster had gone out of his voice.

She didn't want to be the one to tell him, but she saw there was no way out. "Melanie was killed last night," she said gently. "I'm sorry."

Whatever he'd been expecting, it wasn't that. The color drained from his face. His hands gripped the car door as though to keep him from falling.

"Melly? Dead?"

"You knew her well?"

O'Shea ran a hand over his sweat-beaded forehead. "Since she was a toddler, sure. Sixteen years now. Whitman tried to buy me out back then, wanted to gobble up the entire block, he did. I refused—I built my house with my own hands back in 1959, and he was going to raze it so he could put in a tennis court—but after we agreed to disagree, I tried to get along with the man. Melanie was a sweet-tempered child. I can't . . . Melly is dead? How did it . . . what happened? An accident?"

Sydney put her hand on one of his. "She was murdered, Mr. O'Shea."

"Murdered?"

"Last night. She was walking on the campus of the private school she'd been attending, and someone attacked her."

His eyes wandered towards the Whitman house. "That son of a bitch."

"What?"

"If he'd let her live here—her own home, by God—this wouldn't have happened."

It had occurred to her that with Melanie of

driving age and in possession of her own car, and with a housekeeper living on the premises, there was no obvious reason why she wasn't living at home.

"Why wouldn't he let her stay at home?" she asked.

"Because he's a blueblood asshole. Rich men's kids go away to school. His parents had shipped *him* off to some la-de-da boarding school, so he sent her away."

"But not far," she said. "She was close enough to come home for the summer and holidays."

A pained look settled on his face. "And spend the days with old Brunhilda?"

"Whitman isn't around much, I take it?"

O'Shea snorted. "He manages to be elsewhere most of the year. I understand he was in town for two days in April, but I didn't see hide nor hair of him. And I see most everything that goes on around here."

She believed him.

"Melly wasn't allowed home then, either," he continued. "If you want my opinion, it bothers him to see her. The little gold diggers he seems to attract aren't . . . weren't much older than her, and I think having a teenage daughter was an embarrassment to him."

"When did you last see Melanie?"

"At Christmas. She and a couple of her friends came by, gave me plate of cookies she'd baked all by herself." His expression softened. "Those were the worst cookies I ever tasted. I ate every last one of them."

Sydney squeezed his hand. "She was lucky to have a friend like you, Mr. O'Shea."

"No," he said, lowering his eyes. "I was the lucky one."

They fell silent.

After a moment, he cleared his throat. "You said you wanted to ask questions about Melanie. Are you a reporter?"

"I'm a private investigator."

He did not seem surprised. He glanced at the patrol car. "Are you working with the police?"

"No."

"But you're going to try and find whoever killed Melly?"

"I hope so."

He nodded. "If there's anything I can do to help . . ."

"There might be, Mr. O'Shea."

"Just say the word."

It was a long shot, but she asked anyway. "Do you happen to know Melanie's mother's name?"

His face fell. Maybe he'd been expecting her to enlist him in the search for the killer, so he could exact his own revenge. "Her mother?"

"Did Melanie ever mention her?"

"No, I can't say she did. You mean, the mother's alive? I always sort of assumed that it was one of those died-in-childbirth kind of things. It's a sensitive subject, and I never wanted to bring it up."

"I understand."

"Is it important? Maybe I can give Brunhilda one of my super martinis and try to loosen her tongue." He frowned, clearly doubtful. "Or a pitcher of martinis. It might work."

"That's all right. I have other sources," she said, thinking of Mitch.

"But I meant what I said about helping."

"I know. Call me if you remember anything, or if you hear anything." She gave him one of her business cards. "And you've helped already, more than you know."

CHAPTER TWELVE

The police officer was still inside the Whitman residence when Sydney drove off.

She wondered about that. What was he doing in there that would take so long?

If it had been a plainclothes cop she would have understood the length of his stay. A detective would want to go through Melanie's room to search her belongings for anything that might shed some light on her life and death: a diary, an address book, letters, photographs, or anything else they could find.

But would they have sent a patrolman to do a homicide detective's job?

It didn't seem likely.

She turned right onto La Jolla Boulevard and drove, considering it. So absorbed was she in thought, she missed her turn onto Pearl Street and found herself on Prospect.

Summer traffic was heavy in La Jolla—mostly upscale tourists looking for parking places for their BMWs and Mercedes—and it took half an hour to inch through the prime shopping area.

As she passed the third or fourth ice cream parlor along the way, her stomach reminded her that she hadn't eaten. She glanced at her watch. She had two hours remaining before it was time to pick Nicole up from school.

Lunch would have to wait.

She needed to talk to Mitch.

Back in her office, Sydney called the police station and was on hold for five minutes before Mitch came on the line.

"Travis," he said.

She heard in his voice he was not having a good day. "Mitch, it's—"

"Where the hell did you disappear to last night? And why didn't you return my call?"

"I took Nicole home. She was exhausted."

"Well that's just great. Nice of you to take it upon yourself to run this case. You're lucky I didn't send somebody to bring you back."

Sydney resisted the impulse to match his hostility and spoke quietly. "She's fifteen years old, Mitch, and I didn't think she needed to hear some of the things being said in that room."

"All the same, you should have consulted with me. I don't like not knowing what the hell is going on under my own damn nose."

"There's nothing I can do about it now."

"Hmm."

"And," she pointed out, "I'm returning your call right now."

"Twelve hours later."

She raised her eyes toward the ceiling. "Give me strength."

"What was that?"

"Nothing. Just talking to myself." He could be the most exasperating man. "What did you want? Other than to read me the riot act."

His voice changed then. "Sorry kid. I didn't mean to jump down your throat."

"It doesn't matter—"

"But you do. Matter to me."

He was also persistent. Whenever they spoke, sooner or later, it came to this. "Mitch . . ."

"I know. Stick to business." He laughed, but it was an intimate just-between-us laugh. "It's always business with you."

"It always is. So . . . how are things progressing with the Whitman case?"

"They're not."

Sydney had picked up a pencil to take notes and she frowned, tapping the point on the desktop. "What do you mean?"

"We've got nothing. Outdoor scenes are always a bitch to work, and this one was worse than usual. The sprinklers went on while the technicians were trying to collect evidence, and no one could figure out how to turn the damn things off. They run on some kind of timer."

"Oh, no."

"Whatever was there is gone. Bloodstains. Footprints, if there were any. Fibers. What we have now is a lot of mud and trampled grass."

"I hope this happened after the coroner had removed the girl's body?"

"Yes, but just."

"What about on her person?"

"It's too early to say."

"And you didn't find a weapon?"

"Listen, Sydney, I don't think I want to talk about this on the phone. Or at all."

She hesitated, knowing he had no obligation to tell her anything. She considered that on occasion in the past, he'd used the lure of inside information to tempt her into meeting with him.

Was that what he wanted now?

While it had lasted, their affair had been an all-consuming fire. At first glance into those hazel eyes, she'd known he was wrong for her, would be bad for her, might even destroy her; but she hadn't been able to resist his relentless pursuit.

And after he had touched her, nothing else had mattered: not that he was a cop and she was too smart to get involved with a cop; not that he'd been Ethan's partner and Ethan was bound to hear.

Even finding out—some time later—that he was married hadn't been enough to keep her away, although she wanted it to be.

The truth was, being alone with him frightened her and excited her, and she didn't love him anymore. Couldn't love him anymore.

Would *not* love him anymore.

"Maybe we could have dinner," she said.
He didn't even hesitate. "Maybe we could."

For a long time after she hung up the phone, she just sat, staring out the window.
Who was using who, she wondered.
But did it really matter?

CHAPTER THIRTEEN

Shortly after three o'clock, Sydney arrived at Hilyer Academy to wait for Nicole.

They'd agreed last night while they were making plans that Nicole would try to introduce her to Melanie's teachers after school let out so she could set up appointments to interview them. She'd initially thought it preferable to conduct the interviews off campus, and, considering Miss Delacourt's stated intention not to cooperate, it had been the right decision.

The teachers might talk more freely out from under the watchful eyes of the headmistress.

Nicole had also promised to try and arrange a meeting with Terri Allison, if Terri had even been allowed to go to class.

Sydney stood next to the Mustang, drumming her fingers on the roof. The sun was bright this afternoon. The contrast in the light between indoors and out would allow a person standing a certain distance back from a window to see her without her seeing him or her.

She had no doubt Lillian Delacourt knew exactly where that certain distance was, and was at this moment watching her.

If she *really* was a wiseass private eye, she would wave now. A jaunty little wave as if to say, I know you're there; I know you don't like it that I'm here; but what can you do about it?

Miss Delacourt had to be wondering whether it had been Ted Halpern who'd hired her. Sydney wanted her to wonder. She would be leery of taking any action that might upset a parent, in particular one who was concerned with protecting his child.

The kids she could handle—by intimidation it appeared—but a parent might actually talk to the other parents, or even to the school's board of directors, and that wouldn't do at all.

The board of directors might already be thinking of finding someone to blame. And although she didn't look the part, the headmistress would make a very visible sacrificial lamb.

When push came to shove, Lillian Delacourt had to watch her own back.

Who knew what enemies she'd made?

Unlike at public high schools which seemed to erupt with students at the end of the day, only a dozen or so girls straggled out of the building at the final bell. There was one group of four who talked among themselves as they headed for the parking lot, but the others walked alone.

Nicole was the last one out.

Sydney called, "Nicole!"

Nicole looked up and gave a halfhearted wave, then glanced back at the school where the door was closing slowly. She hefted her backpack up onto her shoulder and quickened her pace.

"Sydney," she said a little breathlessly as she came up to the car. "They're coming."

"The teachers?"

Nicole nodded. "Three of them, anyway." Her attention was drawn to where the group of four girls were standing around a Volkswagon Rabbit. "Seniors."

Sydney followed Nicole's eyes. The girls were putting the convertible top down, and were making a show of it. They noisily piled into the car, one of them climbing over the door and into the back seat with a flash of tanned thigh and lacy underwear.

Somehow seniors in high school were looking younger to her every year.

The car pulled away with a lurch—the driver apparently hadn't quite mastered the clutch yet— and Sydney turned back to Nicole, who was watching avidly and a bit enviously as the car left the grounds.

"Melanie wasn't like them," Nicole said. "Melanie wasn't a snob."

Sydney didn't comment. She was inclined to believe Nicole's judgment about Melanie Whitman, but she also knew that it was human nature to idealize someone who has died. At Nicole's age, given the excesses of youth, idealization often became deification.

Thus did a seventeen-year-old murder victim become Saint Melanie.

"Did you talk to Terri?" Sydney asked, hoping to change the subject.

"No. She wasn't in class. Someone said she'd cried all night long. But I got a note up to her, asking her to call me. I gave your number."

"Good."

Nicole opened the passenger door and put her backpack behind the seat. She looked again toward the school. "They should be coming out any minute now. Mr. Anderson, Miss Lockwood, and Mr. King. Only Miss Delacourt called everybody—the teachers, I mean—into her office right after the bell rang."

Sydney could guess why.

"I tried to get Mrs. Dillon too, but she was out sick today."

"Did you tell them what this was about?"

"They knew." Her expression reflected a new awareness, that of a child discovering adults did indeed have an information network of their own. And even—horrors—that it might be more secret and comprehensive than their own.

It was a good sign, Sydney thought, that the teachers were at least willing to talk to her. Of course, that might change, depending on what was being said in Miss Delacourt's office.

"It was terrible in there today," Nicole said. "And so quiet. Quieter than I ever would believe it could be. I could hear the seconds ticking on the clock. A lot of the girls were crying."

"I can imagine."

"I didn't, though."

"No?"

Nicole shook her head. "I think people cry when they feel helpless, when they can't *do* anything else. I'm doing something."

"Yes, but—"

"There they are," Nicole said.

Sydney looked in the direction Nicole's eyes were indicating.

They had come out a side door, one Sydney hadn't known existed, and were walking toward the parking lot. As promised, there were three of them.

CHAPTER FOURTEEN

The first was a man perhaps in his middle thirties. He was dressed in charcoal grey slacks, a white shirt, loafers, and, although it was warm out, a heavy cardigan sweater of brown, tan and red. The bulk of the sweater made him look even shorter and stockier than he was. He had brown hair, wore glasses and had a high forehead.

If she'd seen him on a street somewhere, Sydney would have immediately placed him as a teacher.

The second man she most definitely would not.

Although not particularly tall—perhaps five foot nine—the second man carried himself assertively, with the inborn assurance of someone who looks like a Greek god and damn well knows it.

He was blond, and even at a distance she could see the dark blue of his eyes. His face might have been sculpted by Michelangelo.

He was, in a word, beautiful, as sometimes only men can be.

In white pleated pants and a black shirt, he

belonged on a movie screen, the cover of a magazine, or a poster on a teenaged girl's wall.

What did he teach, she wondered; or rather, what did his students learn? How to look at him with lowered eyes? How to "accidentally" touch his hand when he passed out class assignments?

"Chemistry," Nicole said, as if she knew at least half of what Sydney was thinking. "Chemistry, biology and math."

There were no teachers like him when she was growing up. She'd learned what little she learned about biology from old Mr. Downs, who used to sit and pluck the hairs from his nose with a pair of tweezers during tests.

She looked next at the woman, who was following a few feet behind the men.

Of the three of them, it was the woman she'd be most worried about meeting in a dark alley. Not that she was unattractive, but rather there was, in her stride, something suggesting a latent Marine.

She was wearing a sleeveless knit dress, and her bare arms had more definition than either of the men's. The calves of her tanned legs were thickly muscled.

She had a sharp face, her features cutting. A caricaturist would draw her as a fox. Her short-cropped hair was streaked with blond, and her eyes were an improbable shade of green.

At odds with her athletic appearance was her careful, even artful, use of makeup. It almost, but not quite, hid the lines at the corners of her eyes. She, too, was in her thirties, but clearly intended to fight it every step of the way.

"Nicole," the first man said, and smiled a little sadly. "Here we are, as promised."

"Mr. Anderson, this is Sydney Bryant."

They shook hands. His grip was as solid and sturdy as he was.

"Mr. Anderson teaches English and literature," Nicole added. "Melanie was his best student."

"Now, Nicole," Anderson said, "you know I would never pick a student as the best."

Sydney noticed he'd colored a bit, his neck flushing a none-too-subtle pink.

"But she was your favorite," Nicole insisted. "Everyone knows."

Anderson's eyes met Sydney's for a second and he looked away. "She was a good writer, very serious. And talented."

"Extremely talented," the second man agreed.

A look passed between the two men. It happened so fast that if she'd blinked she would have missed it; but she saw in an instant the fury in Anderson's eyes, and the mild amusement greeting it.

"I had Melanie in chemistry and math," the Greek god said. He held out his hand. "I'm Jeff King."

"Mr. King."

"Jeff." He smiled at Nicole. "Everyone calls me Jeff, isn't that right, Nicole?"

"Right."

"Was Melanie talented in math and chemistry as well?" Sydney asked.

"Very." He smiled again. "She was having a little trouble in chemistry this quarter, but she'd put in some extra time, and I think she'd have

99

pulled off another A." He glanced at Nicole again.

Playing to an audience?

"You were her lab partner," King said to Nicole. "You know how hard she worked."

Nicole returned his smile, but said nothing.

The woman, who'd been listening to all of this without expression, made an effort to smile too, as though including herself in the conversation. She stepped forward. "I'm Sandra Lockwood, and I teach p.e., or what they call p.e. these days. Tennis and swimming and aerobics."

King laughed, put his arm around her shoulder and gave her a quick hug. "Sandy hasn't forgiven the Board for ruling out an obstacle course."

"Jeff," she said, and pushed him half-heartedly away.

"Put a little mud on their faces and make them crawl through barbwire," he went on. "Give them a *real* physical education."

The words were spoken so quietly, she thought she'd imagined them, but when Sydney glanced at Anderson she knew she hadn't.

"Like you do?" he'd said.

But neither Jeff King, nor Sandra Lockwood appeared to have heard. They were looking at each other. Anderson was watching them both, and Sydney could almost feel the tension radiate from him.

Something was definitely going on here.

Nicole turned abruptly on her heel. "I'll wait in the car," she said as she passed Sydney.

Her leaving effectively silenced them.

Jeff King ran a hand through his blond hair. He looked even better disheveled. "Shit," he said, "what's the matter with me? I forgot."

Anderson thrust his hands in his pockets. "Why worry about it? Just smile and I'm sure no one will hold it against you, Jeff. No one ever does." His own smile was thin.

"Shut up, Mark," Sandra Lockwood said, and turned to Sydney. "Miss Bryant, Nicole said you wanted to talk to us about Melanie. What exactly do you want to know?"

"A number of things, actually." She made a point of meeting each one's eyes in turn. "You were her teachers. This is a small school. So I assume you are close to the students, and perhaps know them better than might ordinarily be the case."

"Some of us do," Mark Anderson said.

Sandra Lockwood glared at him.

"I'm interested in what happened yesterday up to the time Melanie was killed. Everything that happened, but specifically anything that might relate to what she was doing that last hour."

Jeff King reached down and picked up a small smooth stone from among the gravel. He rolled it between his thumb and forefinger. "She was studying, wasn't she? With Nicole?"

"And Terri," Sandra Lockwood added.

They were well informed, Sydney thought. "That's right, but only until seven or so. Then she said she had something to do and went off on her own."

Mark Anderson cleared his throat. "And?"

"And I wondered if any of you might know what it was she had to do."

No one spoke. A black Lincoln turned from the

101

road onto the school property, and headed slowly towards them. Sandra Lockwood shaded her eyes with her hand, watching it as it neared.

"Are we suspects?" she said without taking her eyes from the car.

Sydney found that to be an interesting response. "Not really, but why do you ask?"

"My mother didn't raise any fools."

Anderson made a sound of disbelief. "If you have nothing to hide, why—"

He broke off in mid-sentence as the Lincoln entered the parking lot, and parked a few feet away from them. The man who got out wore a clerical collar.

"The Reverend Wolfgang Hauff," Anderson said to Sydney as he approached.

The Reverend Hauff looked as though he had the corner on solemnity. He had the unfurrowed brow of one for whom redemption is guaranteed, along with the ruddy complexion of a fisherman. Although otherwise ascetically thin, he had a potbelly which intimated that he was not above all temptation.

"Good afternoon," he said gravely, and nodded as he passed.

The others nodded in return. Sydney saw on their faces that they disliked the man.

But there seemed to be little love lost between any of them, with the probable exception of Sandra Lockwood for Jeff King.

An interesting group of people, she thought. Interesting, indeed.

CHAPTER FIFTEEN

Sydney made appointments to see Mark Anderson on Saturday morning, Sandra Lockwood that afternoon, and last, but she suspected not least, one for Sunday morning with Jeff King.

"Well?" Nicole said when she got in the car. "What do you think?"

Sydney fastened her seatbelt before answering. "I think Sandra Lockwood has the hots for Jeff King."

"Everyone in school knows *that,* but that wasn't what I meant. What I want to know is, do you think one of them . . . did it?"

She looked at Nicole, surprised. "I wasn't aware you suspected your teachers."

"I don't, really, but I remember you told me once the cops pretty much suspect everybody until they find out otherwise."

"That's true."

"So I guess the only one I know for sure didn't do it is myself."

"I see." She turned the key in the ignition and glanced in the rearview mirror before backing out. In the mirror she saw Jeff King's red Porsche stopped along the drive while he talked to one of the security guards Lillian Delacourt had hired.

The pay for teachers must be getting better, she thought. Even a used Porsche cost a lot of money; add the insurance and upkeep, and owning one would be out of most people's range.

"For all I know," Nicole was saying, "the dragon lady herself might have done it."

"You're referring to Miss Delacourt?"

"If the scales fit . . ."

Sydney laughed softly. "You really don't like her, do you?"

"Does it show?"

"A little." She drove past King's car and saw that the security guard was a woman. It figured.

"I mean, all she ever thinks about is appearances. What would people think. What would people say."

"She's not alone. And," she added mildly, "there are worse ways to be."

Nicole sighed. "I know. But if appearance is all that counts, what's the point of doing more than acting nice, or acting smart, or acting *human?*"

"Well, there is a point. You do it for yourself, to live with yourself."

"Exactly! I want to be as smart as I can be, to learn as much as I can, and *she* worries because I can't balance a book on my head when I walk. That's not what books are for. Or what my head is for."

"Don't worry, Nicole." She glanced sideways at the girl. "You're bright and inquisitive and anyone who knows you, knows it's not an act."

Nicole couldn't hide her pleasure at the compliment. "Tell the dragon lady."

"Maybe I will."

Nicole was silent for a moment and then she shook her head. "I guess I don't really think Miss Delacourt did it, but not because she isn't capable of doing it. She can't stand the thought that she can't control what's happening now. She can't stand knowing it's all out of her hands."

It might well be slipping through Lillian Delacourt's fingers, Sydney thought, but the headmistress was not about to let go without a fight.

The phone was ringing when they arrived at Sydney's apartment, and Sydney left the door open as she went to answer it.

"Yes?"

"Sydney? Is that you?"

"Valentine," she said with some astonishment. She couldn't recall Ethan's secretary ever calling her at home before. "Hello."

"Is Ethan there?"

Nonplused, it took her a few seconds to formulate a reply. "No, he isn't. Why would he be? Isn't he in court?"

"Court recessed early. The judge had a toothache or some such nonsense." Valentine Lund's sense of justice had apparently been affronted.

"Ethan said he was going to stop by your apartment to see you. He informed me that he would be there by four, and it's past four now."

"Well, he's not here yet—"

"Yes, I am."

Sydney turned. Ethan stood in the doorway, a large white paper bag in his arms. "Yes, he is." She held the phone out to him.

He gave her the bag and took the phone in exchange. "Valentine, what is it?"

The tantalizing aroma of Chinese food coming from the bag made her mouth water. Nicole, who'd disappeared into the kitchen, came out with an apple which was quickly forgotten when she smelled the food.

"Wow! Chinese?" She peeked into the bag. "I love Chinese. There's enough here for an army. What are you guys gonna eat?"

Sydney handed the bag to Nicole. "Take it into the kitchen, will you? I need to talk to Ethan."

"Sure. I'm so hungry . . ."

Sydney sat down on the couch and waited patiently until Ethan was off the phone.

"Sorry about that," he said as he hung up. "I told her I was taking the afternoon off, but I don't think she believed me."

"*I* don't believe it." He was, even more than she, a workaholic.

"Well I figured, if you won't come to dinner, dinner would have to come to you."

"Ethan . . ."

"That's all right, Sydney, you don't have to thank me. Although I know for a fact your mother taught you better."

He took off his jacket, draped it over the back of the couch and began to roll up his shirt sleeves. His shirt was damp and she watched the play of muscle beneath it as he moved. "Ethan."

"What?"

"I can't have dinner tonight."

"Sure you can. Unless Nicole eats it all before we get in there."

"I have plans for this evening."

"Oh. Oh!" Awareness dawned in his eyes. "Hmm. A date?"

"I'm sorry." She hated this. "I don't know what to say."

"You don't have to say anything." He smiled and she could see that he meant it. "What about Nicole? Do you want me to stay? Not that a fifteen year old needs a babysitter, but I've got nothing else to do. I'd be glad to keep her company."

"She told me she wanted to go to bed early. I guess she didn't sleep well last night."

"Uh, huh. Well, all dressed up with no place to go. And, sad to say, the story of my life." He reached for his jacket.

"Have dinner with Nicole," she urged, getting to her feet and taking the jacket from him. "And give me a rain check?"

He lifted her chin with one finger and smiled into her eyes. "Absolutely."

She left them to their dinner and went in to shower. With the water beating down, she leaned

107

against the cool tile and fought back the urge to pound her fists on the wall.

Which was worse?

Rushing Ethan out of the apartment, or having him there when Mitch arrived?

With any luck, Mitch would be late.

CHAPTER SIXTEEN

Nicole was alone in the living room watching the five o'clock news on television when Sydney came in after she'd finished dressing.

"Wow, Sydney, you look great."

"Thanks." It was the first time she'd worn the dress, a black silk with a scalloped skirt. The neckline was a bit low for her taste. When she moved a certain way, it showed a hint of white lace and more than a hint of her.

"Umm, Sydney?"

"Yes?"

"Does Ethan know?"

"Know what?"

"That you're . . . who you're . . . you know. I mean, you and Ethan are—"

"Very good friends."

"Right. Good friends. But does he know?"

The kitchen door swung open and Ethan walked in, a glass of iced tea in each hand. "Do I know what?" he asked. He stopped and blinked.

"Whoa! I think it's illegal to look that good. You could get arrested."

"Oh, no," Nicole said, "and you're going out with a—" Her mouth closed suddenly as she looked from Sydney to Ethan and back again. "I mean, without a coat. You'd better wear a coat."

"It's June," Ethan said. "I think she can get by without one."

Sydney smiled at Nicole to show that no harm had been done.

Nicole kept her composure while she accepted the glass of tea Ethan offered and raised it to her lips. But when Ethan turned away, she lowered the glass, crossed her eyes, and drew a finger across her throat.

It was hard not to laugh.

The doorbell rang, and her desire to laugh disappeared.

She steeled herself and went to the door.

Mitch had been facing away from the door, but he turned as it opened. With his dark good looks, dressed in a black suit and ice-blue shirt, he reminded her of Hollywood's version of a Mafia hitman.

He held her evening newspaper out to her. "We didn't make the news," he said, his eyes taking her in, then added, "yet."

"Come in for a minute and say hello to Nicole and Ethan."

She had to hand it to him: he didn't react at all when he heard Ethan's name. Instead, he took two or three steps into the apartment, smiled at Nicole and nodded politely at Ethan.

For his part, Ethan only raised an eyebrow.

"Ethan."

"Mitch."

"It's been a while," Mitch said.

Ethan's expression suggested that he thought it hadn't been long enough.

Her eyes wide, Nicole might have been watching a tennis game as she looked back and forth.

"How's the law practice coming?"

"I can't complain."

"Glad to hear it although I was always surprised you didn't go into criminal law. I'd think the other would be a little tame by comparison."

Ethan smiled thinly. "It's saner, that's for sure. I don't miss the bad guys."

"No, I guess you wouldn't."

Sydney caught the subtle emphasis on *you* in Mitch's tone of voice. Who'd have thought, looking at them now, that once upon a time these two had depended on each other for their very lives?

Apparently Ethan had heard it as well. "How is it on the street these days? Or do they have you pushing papers since you made lieutenant?"

The corner of Mitch's mouth quirked. "No, I just deliver them." He offered the newspaper to Sydney for the second time.

This time she took it.

"I think we'd better go," she said.

At the door she hesitated and turned to look at Ethan. She could feel the heat of Mitch's hand on the small of her back. "Ethan—"

Mitch cut in. "Don't wait up," he said.

"Did you have to say that?" she asked when the door was closed behind them.

"Say what?"

"'Don't wait up'?"

Mitch laughed. His fingers flexed against her back. "Why not? You don't want Nicole staying up all night, do you?"

"We both know you didn't mean that for Nicole."

"Didn't I?"

If his innocent look could be bottled, she thought, the district attorney's conviction rate would plummet, but *she* wasn't buying it.

"You didn't. And we won't be out all night. Or at least I won't."

"'Wherever thou goest . . .'"

CHAPTER SEVENTEEN

Somehow Mitch had gotten reservations at Top O' the Cove. For a Friday night and on short notice that ranked just shy of a miracle.

The true miracle was that he had gotten the famous table six for them. An intimate booth for two, it overlooked La Jolla Cove and was far and away the most romantic setting of any restaurant in town.

The ocean view was spectacular, and for a few minutes she was content to stare in silence at the swell of the waves. Further out, two sailboats skimmed the water's surface, racing each other, but driven by the same wind.

Sydney could almost hear the sound of wind billowing the sails, and smell the fresh salt air, and feel the bite of sea spray on her face.

So entranced was she that it was some time before she became aware that Mitch was watching her instead of the view.

His smile was not the guarded one he usually

wore, but that of a man with his beloved.

There was nothing of the hostility he used as a shield against the world, nor was there the distance she'd often sensed in him.

It was a smile she hadn't seen in a long time, and despite her resolve, something deep inside her stirred in return.

It scared the hell out of her.

"Mitch," she said, and realized she didn't know what to say. As luck would have it, the waiter arrived, saving her from having to say anything for the time being.

They ordered dinner from an eclectic menu which tonight included venison and buffalo. The wine steward brought a cabernet sauvignon. Mitch tasted it and nodded his approval.

"I shouldn't," she said when the steward had gone, but she took a cautious sip. Red wine went to her head even faster than white. It also had the unfortunate effect of making her blush, and she could feel her face warm with just that little sip.

"It looks good on you," Mitch said.

She put down the glass and shook her head. "It's dangerous stuff."

"But in the right hands?"

It wasn't the cabernet deepening her blush. Her mind had betrayed her, playing back a night long ago when the wine had been the least intoxicating thing they'd shared.

His hands, she thought, and looked away.

"I can still taste your bare skin," he said, so softly she almost didn't hear, but she knew he'd intended for her to remember.

114

She hated herself for the shiver that ran down her spine. "Don't."

"What's wrong, Sydney?"

She met his eyes and saw the challenge in them. "Are you afraid?"

"No," she lied. "Why should I be? It's been over for a long time."

"You can say whatever you want, but saying it doesn't make it the truth."

She regarded him with some annoyance. "You're very sure of yourself."

"I am. I have to be, for both of us."

His smile taunted her, and she sought refuge in the view. Gradually, the strains of the classical music in the background drifted into her consciousness.

Combined, the beauty of the seascape and the music of Mozart began to relax her.

For once, Mitch let it go.

"So," he said a little while later. "What do you want to know?"

She glanced up from her salad. "What?"

Now his smile teased. "You agreed to have dinner so you could dig some kind of information out of me. I'm offering to give it to you."

"Why be so cooperative?"

Mitch laughed. "I can't win with you, can I?"

"I'm trying to figure this out. I mean, I've come to you before, and you've told me certain things off the record, but—"

"—not without making you work for it."

Sydney inclined her head in agreement. "Why is this time different?"

"It just is."

He wasn't going to give her a straight answer, she could tell. There was nothing to be gained by pursuing it. "All right," she said, "Melanie Whitman."

"Fine. Ask your questions."

She laid down her fork, the salad forgotten. "Cause of death?"

"Massive head trauma. Her skull was fractured in two places. Right and left. He must have caught her going down with a backswing."

Sydney winced at the image that presented. "Was she sexually assaulted?"

"The medical examiner's report says no. But she wasn't a virgin, either."

"Did she try to defend herself?"

"I doubt if she got close enough. There was no skin or blood under her fingernails, no fiber evidence on her hands."

"All the blood was hers?"

"Hers," he agreed.

That was too bad; advances in science now allowed criminologists to "fingerprint" blood by scrutinizing its DNA. A drop of the killer's blood could provide the forensic scientist with that person's genetic code, and thus identify—or eliminate—a given suspect with a high degree of certainty.

"Did they find any foreign material in the wounds?"

"A little dirt, which probably got there when she

fell. Whatever the killer used to hit her with, it's still intact. We think maybe a baseball bat, but there were no chips or splinters in the scalp or skull."

Sydney frowned. "He must have gotten blood on himself, though."

"The splatter patterns would indicate he did. There was a fine mist of blood on a tree about ten feet away to the left, less to the right—we assume the killer was right-handed—although it pretty much splattered the grass in every direction. That is, it did until the damned sprinklers washed it away."

"He put a lot of force behind the blows."

It was not a question, but he answered anyway. "He loosened her teeth."

"God."

The waiter picked that moment to arrive with the entree and take away her unfinished salad. She looked at the food but had no appetite.

Mitch, ever pragmatic, seemed not to share that particular problem. He cut into the venison and began to eat.

She was aware how incongruous it was to be discussing violent death in these surroundings, but the booth sheltered them and it was unlikely anyone would overhear. Even so, it felt wrong somehow.

Wrong or not, she had to know all of it.

"Where does that leave you?" she asked. "What have you got to go on?"

"Not much. We assume the killer was right-handed. That limits it to the majority of the population. Not exactly a breakthrough. We assume the killer was a male, but a strong woman could have done it. A baseball bat is a great little equalizer."

"But not a woman's weapon." The statistics she'd read on women who murder showed that knives were the weapon of choice, although guns were gaining ground of late.

"You use what you've got on hand. And a baseball bat has an advantage over a knife . . . it gives the killer some distance."

"And distance is an advantage."

"Right." He paused. "There was one thing that was a little odd. The girl was clutching a broken necklace in her right hand. A gold chain."

"And?" she prompted.

"We hoped maybe she'd torn it off the killer—skin works just as well as blood for identifying DNA—but it turned out to be her own. There were marks on her neck where it had been ripped off her."

She considered for a moment. "I don't know what to make of that," she said.

"Neither do I. People have been killed for less than a gold chain, sometimes for the change in their pockets, sometimes for the hell of it, but this felt . . . personal."

"But she held onto it somehow?"

"It was practically embedded in her flesh."

Sydney noticed she'd drawn the waiter's attention. He was looking at her untouched plate. Rather than have him come over to inquire whether her dinner was all right, she began to eat.

"You know I'm working this case," she said.

Mitch didn't look surprised, but he said, "I wish you wouldn't."

"Right now, I wish I wasn't either. I'll try to stay out of your way."

"Who's your client?"

"Halpern," she said, hoping he would assume she meant Nicole's father.

He apparently did. "He's worried about Nicole?"

"Yes."

"I guess I can't blame him, but you know this is my playground."

For some reason that irritated her. "What's the matter, Mitch? Only boys can play?"

"Substitute 'cops' and you've got it."

"Then why are you telling me all of this?" she asked, exasperated.

"I just am."

"Back to that again. All right, you are, so tell me the rest."

"There isn't too much else. We've talked to a few of her friends, the teachers, and no one seems to know anything. She wasn't dating, didn't have a boyfriend anyone knew of, but someone was getting into her pants."

"How delicately put."

"I could be less delicate. Anyway, she spent a lot of time off campus. On Fridays she told the people at school she was going home for the weekend, but she didn't. Likewise, she told the housekeeper she was staying at school on those days, and she wasn't. We don't know where the hell she went."

"Someone has to know."

"If they know, they're not telling us."

Sydney thought she might have better luck, but discretion kept her from saying so.

"We'd put her picture in the paper and ask for the public's help, but we still haven't reached her father to notify him she's dead. Heaven forbid this asshole flies into town, sees his daughter's picture on the front page, and finds out that way. *If* he'd even recognize her, which I wouldn't bet on."

"What about the mother?"

"The mother's dead, too. Committed suicide a couple of years ago."

So there was no family to mourn her.

"And then," he went on, "we've got what happened at the Whitman house."

"What?"

"Sometime last night, someone tossed Melanie's room. And only her room. Searching for something, probably. What they were looking for, I don't know, nor do I know whether they found it."

That explained the police officer this morning. "The same person who killed her."

"That'd be my guess. The evidence technicians are going through the room inch by inch. Maybe they'll have better luck there than at the murder scene."

"Maybe," she said, but she had a strong feeling the answer to the mystery of Melanie Whitman's death would not be found by an evidence technician.

CHAPTER EIGHTEEN

It was eight-thirty by the time they'd finished dinner. The sun had set during dessert, turning the sky into a palette of magnificent color that man could never hope to match.

Pale oyster-pink, ocher, and gold at the horizon, while the blue leaked its essence into the sea.

For a few moments, as the sun hovered at the brink, she'd wished she could follow it, chase after it so it would always be sunset.

She felt a sense of loss when the sun had disappeared.

The loss was transitory. Twilight came, and that and a second glass of wine mellowed her out.

"We'd better go," Mitch said when she'd finished the wine.

The valet brought the car around, and held the door for her. She sank gratefully into the seat and closed her eyes while waiting for Mitch.

When she opened her eyes what felt like scant seconds later, they were turning into the guest parking lot at her apartment.

Mitch parked—crookedly, she noticed, the way most cops parked—and came around to her side of the car to get the door for her. A good thing, since she couldn't figure out how to open it.

"You're not walking straight," he said as they started up the pathway. He put his arm around her.

"I *am* walking straight."

"That's what they all say. Do you want me to give you a sobriety test?"

She swallowed a laugh. "I can't pass that sober. I don't even have a number two pencil."

"Then behave." He pulled her closer to him.

"Mitch," she said. She wasn't sure what was wrong here, but something was. An alarm was going off somewhere in her head.

"Ssh. The neighbors will hear you."

"It isn't exactly the middle of the night. Is it?"

They stopped at the security gate and he tried it. "It must be after nine, because this gate is locked. Give me your keys."

"You don't have to walk me in."

He took her purse from her. "Sydney, I will see you to your door."

She watched him search for and find the key. A cool breeze had come up. The feel of it on her skin made her shiver.

The fresh air also began to clear her mind.

He gave her back her purse, then held the gate for her as she stepped through. They walked into the courtyard side by side, but he made no move to

122

put his arm around her again. As they neared her wing of the complex, she saw that the windows of her apartment were dark. Nicole had apparently gone on to bed.

"Well," Mitch said when they'd reached the door. "Here we are."

"Yes."

He still had her keys and he unerringly selected the one to the front door, but didn't use it. "I don't suppose you're going to invite me in?"

"I don't think that would be a good idea."

"Might I ask why?"

"You know why." She reached for her keys; he closed his fingers around them.

"Then why don't we go away?"

"Mitch . . ."

"What do you say? A weekend in Catalina? We could spend all day in bed."

"No."

He smiled knowingly. "But you're tempted?"

"No, I'm not."

"I don't believe you."

"May I have my keys?"

"In a minute." He slipped them into his pocket and leaned one shoulder against the doorframe. "It's not easy getting you alone."

Sydney took a step back. "This is not the way to do it."

"I know the way to do it."

"Oh, now you sound like a twelve year old trying to convince his friends."

"I shouldn't have to convince you," he said.

"What is this? Are you fishing for compliments? All right, then, you were awesome. Totally awesome. There aren't even words to describe how wonderfully awesome you were."

She'd hoped that her sarcasm would bother him, but he only laughed.

"What are you afraid of?" he asked for the second time that night.

"Nothing!"

"Come on, Sydney. You're trembling."

"If I am, it has nothing to do with you."

He reached out with his left hand, touching her face with his fingertips. "No? I think it does. I think you want me."

"Ethan—"

"Ethan's not here," he whispered. "There's no one here to protect you."

"I don't need protection, and I don't need this," she said.

"You're wrong, this is exactly what you need."

She felt a flash of fury, but even as she thought of what to say, it was she who moved towards him.

Somehow her traitorous arms found their way around his neck. Somehow her body molded to his. And somehow his mouth found and claimed hers.

I shouldn't be doing this, she thought.

But the searing heat of him drove all thought from her mind.

The breath left her.

Even with her lungs aching, she made no attempt to pull away, giving herself over to the sensation that began and ended with his touch.

It was he who released her.

For a moment she stood, her eyes closed, unable to move, waiting for him to kiss her again. When he didn't, she finally opened her eyes.

He cupped her face in his hands. "Welcome to the real world, Sydney."

CHAPTER NINETEEN

Saturday, June 11th

Nicole was already up and about when Sydney opened her eyes to the morning light. Her head ached dully and her stomach was the slightest bit queasy, no doubt a legacy of last night's wine.

So much for the real world.

She sat up on the sofa bed and scooted backwards until she could lean against the cushions. She pulled her nightshirt over her legs and hugged them to her, resting her chin on her knees.

And found she was looking at the phone. Should she call Ethan?

No.

Last night after Mitch had left her at the door, she'd wanted almost desperately to hear the sound of Ethan's voice; but as she'd dialed his number she had realized all at once that he couldn't always rescue her. And that he shouldn't have to.

She'd hung up the phone.

Three years ago when she'd sent Mitch back to his wife, Carol, Ethan had been her lifeline, the anchor of her resolve. He'd accompanied her to his family's second home down in Mexico, where she'd spent a week coming to terms with her feelings.

Feelings which she had kept under tight control until last night.

Her control had slipped, but she couldn't keep running to Ethan—*save me from the big, bad policeman*—because it wasn't fair to either of them.

She'd have to work this out herself.

"You're up?" a voice said from behind her.

Sydney looked over her shoulder. Nicole had entered the room from the kitchen, carrying some unidentifiable food on a small plate. She was barefoot, dressed in faded jeans and a red-checkered shirt, and she'd put her long blond hair in pigtails.

"I hope I didn't wake you," Nicole said, delicately picking whatever it was up with her fingers and taking a bite.

"No." Sydney massaged her temples gently. "I've got work to do anyway . . ."

"Terri called last night."

She looked at Nicole with interest. "What did she have to say?"

Nicole perched on an arm of the sofa. "She didn't really say much, or at any rate, nothing that made any sense. She's still pretty upset."

Sydney didn't point out that what might not make sense to Nicole could turn out to be vital information, because it could just as easily not. "Were you able to set a time when I can talk to her?"

Nicole nodded. "Tonight, sometime after six. She and a couple other girls are supposed to be going to a movie—to help take her mind off everything—but they're coming here instead."

"Six," Sydney said, "that's fine." She'd be back from her interview with Sandra Lockwood by then. And she'd have talked to Mark Anderson as well.

Nicole took another bite of what Sydney could now see was a patty of cold egg foo young which she'd folded in half. "The thing is, now I have to go see the movie this afternoon that *they're* supposed to see tonight so I can tell them the plot. That way, if Miss Delacourt asks about it, they can fake her out."

"Oh?"

"Yeah. They're even going to go to the UTC mall and get in the ticket line at the theater. That way, anyone who might be following them will be thrown off track."

Sydney hid a smile. She imagined the University Towne Center mall swarming with teenage girls skulking around in trench coats trying not to be noticed. Still, their willingness to go to such lengths to help was encouraging, considering certain adults in this case had been less than forthcoming thus far.

"The thing is," Nicole went on, "I kind of wanted to come with you."

"Nicole . . ."

"I know. I'd be in the way."

"It isn't that. People are funny . . . sometimes they'll tell someone they hardly know things they'd never dare tell a close friend. If you were with me, I'm sure your teachers would censor themselves."

"But I *know* them. I'll know whether they are telling the truth."

"If it was that easy to judge truthfulness, I'd be out of a job," she said, only half joking. "And you'd have a spot on the Supreme Court."

Resignation showed on Nicole's face. "Okay, all right. I guess I'll stay here and study until it's time to go to the show."

"Will you need a ride to the mall?"

She shook her head. "I'll take the bus." She grinned impishly. "I love to go to the movies, but I don't know how any movie could be better than last night."

The change of subject caught Sydney off guard. "What about last night?"

"Ethan and that police lieutenant. I sure wouldn't mind them fighting over me."

CHAPTER TWENTY

A tropical storm spawned in the Gulf of Mexico had sent tentacles of moist, unstable air into southern California. When Sydney stepped outside, she immediately began to perspire.

To the east, cumulonimbus clouds were gathering, extending high into the sky. The weatherman had promised a fifty-percent chance of thundershowers by evening, and flash flood warnings had been issued for the desert and low-lying areas.

As warm and humid as it already was, Sydney knew it would only get warmer as the day went on. In addition, Mark Anderson lived in Mira Mesa, and the further inland she drove, the hotter it would get.

The Mustang had air conditioning, but there were few things more unappealing than the thought of stepping out of a cool car into the sauna she knew Mira Mesa would be. Except for having to get back in the car after it had sat in the scorching sun for an hour or two.

She went through the gate and turned toward the covered parking area, but stopped after taking a few steps.

There, sitting on the trunk of her car in the shade, was Victor Griffith. He was holding a folded newspaper which he was using to fan himself.

He saw her at the same time she saw him. Escape was impossible.

"Victor."

Griffith slid off the trunk. "I'd come to you, you sweet thing, but I can't stand this damned heat." He crooked a finger at her. "Don't just stand there, Sydney, come on out of the sun."

She walked slowly toward him. "What are you doing here?"

"You always ask me that."

"Because you're always showing up on my doorstep."

He laughed, not nicely. "From the way you said that, I must be like a bad dream."

"The word is nightmare."

"No, it'd be a nightmare if I wore a ski mask and carried a chainsaw." He leered. "And you would be wearing the requisite see-through nightie."

"Victor." There was little difference in temperature under the sheltering roof, but at least the sun wasn't beating down on her. Sydney could feel a trickle of sweat as it ran down her spine. "What—"

"What do I want?"

"Yes. What *do* you want?"

"The same thing I wanted yesterday. Give me

the girl's name and I'll go away. Otherwise . . ." He smiled, the threat implicit.

"Sorry."

"I wouldn't be so quick to say no."

"Don't you have anything better to do? Is it a slow news day or something?"

"Or something. Look at this." He handed her the newspaper.

It had been folded to an inside page. It only took a second before she saw what he meant by 'this.' The article was third in a column of brief local news items:

Slain girl was beaten, autopsy finds

A seventeen-year-old girl killed Thursday on the campus of Hilyer Academy was severely beaten, according to a coroner's autopsy report.

The girl, whose name is being withheld pending notification of relatives, suffered severe head injuries during the attack.

The girl's body was found on a secluded pathway by a classmate, a police spokesperson said.

Sydney frowned. It was a standard tell-nothing item, the like of which had become more frequent as violent crime rose in the city.

"You see what I mean?" Victor took the paper from her and glared at it. "I wrote this shit, and it's damned embarrassing, but there was nothing more to tell. A day and a half later, and there's nothing to fucking tell."

"What does that have to do with me?"

"You know the answer to that. If I had the girl's name, I could do something with this."

She unlocked the car and tossed her purse onto the front passenger seat. "I can't help you. You'll have to wait until the police are ready to release it."

"Listen . . . I can make it worth your while."

"If I were foolish enough to tell you and the police found out I'd leaked it, they'd never trust me with anything confidential again. I shouldn't have to tell you, of all people, how vital it is that I have a source in the department. I can't afford to risk losing it."

"Come on." He made no attempt to hide his disbelief. "Your *source* isn't about to cut you off. Everyone knows you're the fair-haired child as far as Mitchell Travis is concerned."

"Lieutenant Travis isn't running this investigation," she said.

"Not technically, maybe, but he's supervising the homicide team that is. He was at the scene. And he's making a lot of the decisions that are being made."

"Then why don't you ask him?"

"He doesn't like me. Imagine that."

"I'll try."

Griffith took a none-too-clean handkerchief from his pants pocket and drew it across his face. "Anyway, I don't see why you and I can't work together. It could prove to be mutually advantageous."

"Oh? How do you figure that?"

"You tell me some things, I'll tell you some things. A little give-and-take. I haven't exactly been resting on my laurels here."

"What do you know that I'd be interested in?"

"Ah, you forget, I have access to the morgue at the newspaper."

"Is that where they keep dead reporters?"

"It is to laugh. Ha ha. But no, it is a place where old news stories are laid temporarily to rest. Organized in such a way I can search for a name, or a particular subject—say, murder?—or, of course, for what might have happened on a given date."

"But you don't have a name."

"Not *the* name, but I have others."

"What others?"

His eyebrows arched. "Think about it."

Sydney did. There were a lot of names she'd be interested in, some of which might have come to the attention of the news media. It was amazing sometimes how much information could be compiled on an individual without the individual being aware of it.

Lillian Delacourt. Albert Locke Whitman. Jeff King. Sandra Lockwood. Mark Anderson. Wolfgang Hauff. Even grandmotherly Theadora Fairweather.

It could be enlightening to see what their dossiers might contain. All of them except for Whitman, because she'd be giving the game away if she included his name with the others.

Still, she was hesitant. If it had been anyone else offering to share information, she'd have jumped at the chance to pick his brain; but with Victor

Griffith there was no telling what might spew out.

Or what the eventual price might be.

"I can see you have doubts," he said. "All right, I'll give you a sample. A free sample, with no strings attached."

She knew there was no such thing. "Thanks anyway," she said, making a point of glancing at her watch. It was nine-thirty and her appointment with Mark Anderson was for ten. "But I really don't have time." She got into the car.

He held the door, keeping her from closing it. "Not a name, though. The names are too precious. But a place? Say, Hilyer Academy?"

"Victor, let go."

"The student body—and I use the term loosely, though not, perhaps, as loosely as they do—the student body is normally one hundred students. Twenty-five freshmen, twenty-five sophomores, and so on."

"That's fascinating, but I've got to go."

"This January, however, one of the freshmen girls left school because her parents couldn't keep up with the tuition. They preferred to eat, I suppose. But anyway, you can see that the place is ripe with possibilities. Ninety-nine luscious co-eds—"

"They're only coeds if there are male students enrolled in the school too."

He waved that away. "It doesn't matter. They're coeds to me and every B-grade movie producer in Hollywood. Besides, it would ruin my song otherwise."

She thought she might regret it, but she asked

anyway, "Your song?"

He cleared his throat and sang:

"Ninety-nine coeds at Hilyer High,
Ninety-nine coeds at Hilyer,
If one of those coeds should happen to die,
Ninety-eight coeds at Hilyer High."

CHAPTER TWENTY-ONE

Mark Anderson lived in one of the condominium developments which had mushroomed in Mira Mesa over the past few years. What had been open land—albeit, essentially desert—now was covered with six- and eight-hundred square foot condos whose owners invariably commuted to work and clogged the freeways.

On Saturdays, however, they seemed to prefer the streets, and it was after ten when she arrived at Anderson's address. She found a lot marked 'guest parking' and set out to find his unit in the maze.

After circling the man-made pond for the third time—every fork in the path returned sooner or later to the water—she asked directions from a boy on a skateboard who merely pointed at a door some ten feet away from where they were standing.

"What an investigator," she said under her breath as she rang Anderson's doorbell, then turned to admire the mini-waterfall as she waited for him to answer.

"Hello! I'd about given up on you." Mark Anderson pushed open the screen door to allow her to come in. He wore tan slacks and a short-sleeved blue shirt, neither of which had lost their crisply ironed creases in the heat. "You found the place with no trouble?"

She smiled and nodded; let him interpret that any way he wanted. "Thank you for seeing me today."

"No problem."

He led her through the tiny entryway into the small living room where the air was being stirred by an oscillating fan. It wasn't air conditioning, but it was better than nothing.

She looked around the room. By keeping the furniture down to a minimum—a couch, one end table, and two chrome and canvas chairs—he'd managed to make the room look larger than it was. But even so, it was somewhat claustrophobic, as though the earth-tone walls were pressing in.

Stacked on the floor to one side of the couch were the ubiquitous blue books she recalled from her own days in school. A pencil with blue on one end and red on the other sat on top of the pile.

"Welcome to the family estate," he said. He waited until she'd sat on the couch before pulling up one of the chairs, but remained standing. "The maid has the day off, thank God, or we'd be crammed in here like sardines. Would you like something to drink? I make a mean iced coffee."

As a rule, Sydney seldom drank coffee, but all at once it sounded good. Iced anything would have sounded good. "If it's no bother."

"None at all. And—" he crossed the room in four steps and opened a sliding door which revealed a narrow cramped kitchen "—thanks to modern architectural wisdom, we'll be able to talk while I work."

"Then I'd love it."

"Good." He opened the refrigerator freezer, pulled out an old-fashioned metal ice tray and waved it at her. "You know how hard it is to find these things these days? I had to drive all over town. The little plastic jobs that came with the refrigerator make hail-sized cubes, and when you try to get them out by bending the thing, the cubes shoot across the room."

Sydney smiled but didn't comment. Anderson hadn't impressed her as a talkative type yesterday when they'd met, and she wondered whether the prospect of the interview was making him nervous.

"I got the recipe for this from a Thai restaurant in Los Angeles," he said, putting ice cubes in tall glasses. "Even though I was desperately poor, I used to go there every week, mostly for the iced coffee, and they finally took pity on me. I guess the fact I was paying the bill with nickels and dimes and quarters clued them in that I was just scraping by."

"Are you from L.A.?"

He stopped what he was doing and looked at her. "Is that a question or small talk?"

"Both."

"Hmm. Yes. I grew up there." He took a pitcher from the refrigerator and poured a rich dark liquid

141

into the glasses until it was an inch or two from the top. He replaced the pitcher and brought out a carton of milk which he sniffed before adding it to the coffee where it settled to the bottom.

"Do you have family there still?"

"I don't have family anywhere." He brought the glasses into the front room and handed her one, along with a straw. "Now or then. I'm one of those kids who grew up waiting to be adopted, but never was."

"I'm sorry."

"Ah, well."

She studied him for a moment as he unwrapped his straw and plunged it among the ice cubes. She wouldn't have thought he'd come up hard, despite the anger he'd shown towards Jeff King. There was a gentleness about him which seemed at odds with a homeless childhood.

He glanced up and caught her eyes. "Don't waste any sympathy on me, Miss Bryant. That was how I was brought up; but since I didn't know any other way of living, I never knew what I was missing."

"Call me Sydney."

"All right, Sydney. And it's Mark."

She smiled and leaned forward, reaching across to shake his hand. "Mark."

"So . . . you're here to ask me about Melanie."

"Yes. Do you mind if I record our conversation?" She put down the iced coffee and took her microcassette recorder out of her purse.

"Why should I mind?"

"It bothers some people," she said, putting a

new tape into the machine.

"Not me."

When the tape was in place, she pushed the record button and watched for a moment to see if it was at speed. "Okay, I'm set." She smiled to reassure him. "You were Melanie's English teacher, is that right?"

"Yes. And literature."

"I understand the school is set up so there are twenty-five students in each grade."

He nodded, but his eyes widened slightly, as if he hadn't expected her to know or care about such details, and his expression showed a heightened respect.

Thank you, Victor, she thought, for that bit of information. Mark Anderson was a teacher, after all; he would naturally appreciate that she had done her homework.

"Melanie was in the senior class," she said. "Had you taught her for the four years she was at Hilyer?"

"Yes, of course." He smiled. "I teach four periods of English, one for each class level, and two periods of literature. I actually had Melanie in eight classes altogether."

"Nicole seemed to think Melanie was a favorite of yours."

Again the color rose in his face. He raised the straw to his mouth and took a sip of his drink. "I guess she was," he said, finally.

"You knew her very well."

He blinked. "I guess I did."

Sydney regarded him. "You guess?"

"I did."

She waited for him to continue. The tape recorded silence for awhile before he spoke.

"Melanie was an excellent student," he said carefully, "and a talented writer. She often brought her stories to me for critiquing."

"Yes?"

He held his iced coffee in both hands and leaned forward, unmindful of the condensation that was dripping off the glass and onto the beige carpet. "We had a lot in common."

Sydney inclined her head, indicating he should go on.

"That doesn't seem likely, I guess. The daughter of a rich man and someone who had so much of nothing. But if you consider the emotional aspect . . . neither of us had what you'd call a loving upbringing. Quite the opposite. It was something else we shared. Besides the love of the written word."

"So you were more than teacher and student."

"Yes. Friends. We were friends."

"May I ask how your friendship came to be? I assume you aren't that close to all of your students."

He shook his head. "It started with a story she had written. A remarkable story she turned in as a class assignment. It was disturbing, full of not-so-hidden rage, and I thought I should talk to her about it."

"And?" she prompted when he fell silent.

"I asked her to see me after class—this was in her freshman year—and I told her I'd read the story

144

and it was good, but I wondered if a happier ending might not make it better."

Sydney watched as a range of emotion played across his face, from something that might have been nostalgia to sorrow and even regret.

"Melanie said, 'There are no happy endings.'"

Sydney felt a pang of compassion for a thirteen-year-old Melanie who time had proved was right, for herself at least. "What did you say to that?"

"Oh, the right things. I told her there *were* happy endings. And that a lot of young girls felt the way she did, but it wouldn't always be that way." He smiled and rubbed the side of his nose. "I lied, of course."

"Why 'of course'?"

"Do you know anyone who is completely happy?"

She chose not to answer. "Was Melanie satisfied with that?"

"No. She told me—" he smiled again, remembering "—she told me she thought I was smarter than that. I had to laugh. Melanie laughed with me."

It was clear that the memory was a fond one, maybe even a cherished one. "And after that?"

"We talked for a long time. I told her she could always come to me if she had a problem."

"Which I gather she did."

"Over the years, yes. Mostly it was little things; making friends with the other girls, problems with her studies, that type of thing. But also her father . . . you know about the situation?"

"Yes."

"I wasn't sure Lillian would mention it to you. Initially, I was reluctant to tell her, but I thought I shouldn't withhold anything."

"Miss Delacourt didn't mention it. Nicole told me, and I've since talked to a neighbor of Melanie's who said pretty much the same thing."

"Oh?"

She thought she detected a hint of irritation in his voice and wondered at the reason behind it. Was he bothered that the girl had shared her confidences with someone besides himself?

"How did Melanie feel about her father's treatment of her?"

"By the time I met her, I don't think she felt anything at all about it."

"I understand she hadn't seen him since she started at the school."

"That's right. I thought once, before I knew her very well, that I should call him and tell him what he was doing to her by his absence."

"She wouldn't have appreciated that?"

"She'd have hated it. She hated him. Every time a plane went down anywhere in the world, she'd keep her fingers crossed, hoping he'd been on it."

Sydney frowned. She could imagine the girl hating her father, but wishing him dead? "Was she undergoing any counseling?"

"Not that I was aware of. Although she had the opportunity to consult with Wolfgang Hauff if she wished. I don't think she did."

It would be a question to ask the Reverend. "Was she close with any of the other teachers? Might she have confided in them?"

146

His earlier irritation returned in full force. "If you mean Jeff King, I know some of the girls had crushes on him, but Melanie wasn't one of them, regardless of what he might think."

"Tell me about Jeff King," she suggested.

"There isn't much to tell. He's only been at Hilyer for a year. Lillian recruited him shortly after she came. The science teacher prior to King had to be fired . . . he was drinking on the job."

"You don't think much of King."

"I try not to think of him at all."

"Is there a reason why? Is he an incompetent or unethical teacher?"

"I can't say anything about his competence. Science is not my field."

"And his ethics?" A very attractive man among all those teenage girls would undoubtedly be subject to temptation. It would be easy to succumb.

"I don't know."

"Melanie never indicated to you that he was—"

Mark's eyebrows drew together. "No. She saw through him from the first day."

"He seemed to feel they were on good terms," she noted.

"I'm sure," he said dryly, "it has never occurred to Jeff that a female could resist his charms."

"Melanie wasn't attracted to him, I take it."

"No. As a matter of fact, we laughed about him, and the way the other girls were fussing over him. She thought he was in love with himself."

"And what about Melanie? Was she in love with anyone?"

"In love?"

"Was she seeing anyone?"

He couldn't hide his confusion. "Melanie? Seeing anyone? No . . . she . . . I don't think she was seeing anyone. Why do you ask?"

"I've been told that Melanie left campus every weekend."

"Well, yes. She went home. I mean, her father was never there, so it was a kind of refuge for her, to get away from school."

"She told you that?" she asked.

"Yes. Why?"

"Because it isn't true, Mark. No one knows yet where she spent those days, but it wasn't at home. The police have reason to believe she may have been with a lover."

CHAPTER TWENTY-TWO

For a moment Sydney thought Mark would shatter the glass in his hands; his knuckles were white as he tightened his fingers around it.

"A lover? But . . . but how could they . . ."

The words died in his throat. His graying complexion told her he'd figured out how the police might know such a thing.

He got up abruptly, but seemed at a loss as to what to do.

"I'm sorry," she said.

He stared blankly at the floor, the muscles of his jaw tensing with emotion. The glass tilted in his hand, threatening to spill.

Sydney got up from the couch and took the glass from him, placing it on the end table with her own. When she turned towards him again, she saw that his eyes were bright with unshed tears.

"She was a beautiful, sensitive child."

"Not a child," Sydney said quietly. She pushed on his shoulders, wanting him to sit down, and he collapsed into the chair.

"How could anyone do that to her?"

She didn't want to aggravate him any further, but it was her job to ask questions. "By 'that' you mean make love to her?"

"Love?" His laughter sounded harsh. "It isn't love to take advantage of someone."

His attitude was curiously old-fashioned. Surely he must be aware that girls younger than Melanie were not only sexually active these days, but in many cases initiated their intimate relationships. Even with the threat of AIDS, sex among teenagers was rampant.

Now was not the time, she thought warily, to bring those particular facts to his attention.

"She never told you she was seeing anyone?" she asked one last time.

He gave her a wounded look. "No."

In the back of her mind, she wondered at the source of his outrage. Was all of this jealousy? Had he been in love with Melanie Whitman?

She should, she thought, ask him now when his defenses were lowered, but she didn't. He might not even realize how he felt about her. It was possible he'd buried his feelings so deep he didn't know himself.

Instead, she turned off the tape recorder and put it back in her purse.

"Thank you for talking to me," she said. "I'm sorry if what I've told you has upset you, but it's important I learn as much about Melanie as I can."

Mark made a visible effort to pull himself to-

150

gether. "Of course, I . . . I just hate to think she would do something so foolish. It might have ruined her life. She had a future and now . . ."

Now she was dead. Sydney said nothing, because there was nothing to say.

He looked down at his empty hands which he clenched into fists. "Whoever did that to her deserves to have the same done to him."

She hesitated, but went ahead and asked the question which bothered her most of all. "Do you have any idea why someone would want to kill her?"

Mark frowned. "No. But I thought it just happened, didn't it?"

"A police lieutenant told me this murder felt personal to him, and I think I agree with him. But seventeen is kind of young to have someone wanting to kill you, and it makes me wonder."

"You think . . . the police think . . . it was someone she knew?"

"Almost certainly."

Either he was an excellent actor, or the thought had never occurred to him. He opened his mouth to speak, then shut it again.

Sydney could tell his mind was racing, but in the end he only shook his head.

"What she was going to do that night?" she asked. "Or who she was going to see?"

If he knew the answer to either question, Mark Anderson was keeping his peace.

CHAPTER TWENTY-THREE

Sydney left Mark Anderson to his thoughts and headed back towards University City. She had an hour and a half to kill before her one o'clock appointment with Sandy Lockwood, which would allow her time to stop by the office.

As she drove, she reflected on what Mark had said. And on the way he'd said it.

Had he been in love with the girl? Maybe. He'd certainly cared for her deeply. And if he had loved her, it wouldn't be the first time a teacher had fallen in love with a student, nor would it be the last. But had Melanie returned his feelings?

If his stricken response to the news Melanie had had a lover was genuine—and she thought it was—it followed that Mark Anderson hadn't been the one.

Sydney could believe that a gentle man like Mark might fall in love, and seek to keep that love inviolate until the proper time. With the sensibilities of a romantic, he would be willing to deny himself the pleasures of a more physical expression of his feelings.

He was a man who would give the woman he loved a single rose for her to press between the pages of a book of poetry. He would remember how the sunlight caressed her, how the breeze played through her hair.

The woman he loved would always walk in beauty.

That standard of perfection might be difficult for a teenage girl to sustain. And it could get lonely up on a pedestal.

Particularly if someone else was standing in the wings, offering a more earthy appreciation of her feminine charms. Someone who wouldn't want to wait, who would insist he *couldn't* wait.

Sydney remembered very well how it felt to be a teenage girl, the sense of having something men wanted, something they sometimes begged for. It was undeniably a feeling of power.

And what good was having power without using it?

Whatever her feelings for Mark Anderson, at some point, Melanie had found an outlet for that power.

When she arrived at the office, Sydney stopped at Luigi's Deli, ordered a sandwich and a Pepsi, and took them upstairs to eat.

It was warm and stuffy in the office, she turned on the air conditioner, and stood in front of it to cool off. The chilled air did little to dry her damp

154

blouse, but it felt great anyway.

She sat down at the desk and went through the mail while she ate. There wasn't much. A check from a woman whose ex-husband she'd found— he'd been hiding out with an old girl friend, trying to avoid his child support payments—and a post card from her mother.

The postcard showed the New York skyline at dusk. The lights sparkled like diamonds, the way the stars used to when she was a child before city lights had stolen their thunder.

She turned the card over and read:

Sydney,

You notice I sent the card to your office instead of your home. If you're reading this on Saturday, you are spending too much time at work. Go home.

By the way, we've decided to take an extra few days and see *The Phantom of the Opera*. I've spent your inheritance on the tickets.

Love,
Mom

(P.S. Give my love to Ethan.)

Sydney smiled. Her mother had wanted her to go along to New York, and Laura Ross had tried to persuade Ethan he could use a vacation; but Sydney seriously doubted if she and Ethan could keep up with them.

Of course, that may have been the point: remove them from their work, throw them together for a solid week, and leave them alone now and again.

Their mothers made no secret of the fact they wanted Sydney and Ethan to be together. Although Ethan was eight years older than she, that had probably been the plan from the day Sydney was born.

Ethan's short-lived marriage to someone else after Sydney left San Diego to work in a Los Angeles investigative firm had been a mere detour as far as their mothers were concerned.

Sydney's affair with Mitch Travis was also an unfortunate wandering from the chosen path.

She was glad her mother was in New York. Kathryn Bryant had a kind of sixth sense that alerted her whenever Sydney had any contact with Mitch. Her mother never would say anything, but there would be a watchful look in those eyes which were so much like her own.

And after last night . . .

Sydney glanced at the phone. She tapped the edge of the postcard on the desk, considering what to do. She could, she supposed, call Ethan on the chance he didn't know of their mothers' intentions to stay in New York for a few more days.

But no. Her earlier decision had to stand.

If Ethan wanted to talk to her, he knew where to find her.

CHAPTER TWENTY-FOUR

Sandra Lockwood came to the door with a smile that didn't quite reach her eyes. She was wearing a short blue satin robe and her hair was wet, as if she'd just gotten out of the shower.

"Good, you're here," she said, and held the door wide. "I timed that just right."

Sydney stepped inside. "Thank you for seeing me today. I hope I'm not keeping you from something?"

"Not at all. Why don't we talk on the terrace?"

Sydney followed her through a spotless apartment decorated—surprisingly, she thought—in a French provincial style. A thick paperback romance novel, which lay open and face down on the floral divan, was the only sign of habitation, and the only indication this was not a furniture showroom.

The terrace opened off the dining area and was shaded by a row of eucalyptus trees. It was cooler than she'd supposed it would be, and she was grateful. Sydney set the tape recorder on the arm of the chair and turned it on.

"I talked to the police this morning," Sandra Lockwood said as she sat down. Her eyes moved from the recorder to Sydney. "I got the impression they haven't the faintest idea who could have killed Melanie."

"Do you have any idea?"

"Me? No, but I haven't given it much thought." She tucked her bare feet beneath her, and picked at a string on the hem of her robe. "I didn't know Melanie all that well."

"How long have you worked at Hilyer?"

"It was my first job right out of college. I'm thirty-five now, so it's been fourteen years. Fourteen very long years."

"Why so long?"

"It isn't easy working with one hundred prima donnas. I'm sure you are aware by now that most of them come from wealthy families. They hate to sweat. I do believe the little darlings think only poor people are born with sweat glands."

"Was Melanie a prima donna?"

Sandra Lockwood hesitated and then nodded. "She could be very headstrong when it suited her. She enjoyed swimming, played fair tennis, but she always had an excuse not to participate in aerobics. She'd twisted her ankle, or she had a headache, or a stitch in her side."

Judging by her scornful expression, Sydney thought the physical education teacher might not consider a broken leg to be a satisfactory excuse.

"I gave her a C last term. She didn't like that

one bit."

"What about this term? How was she doing?"

"Hmm. About the same. A new set of excuses. But—" Sandra smiled coldly "—the word had come down that she was to receive no lower than a B."

"The word came from whom?"

"Lillian."

"Was she in the habit of telling you how to assign grades?"

"Not usually."

"Did this apply only to Melanie, or were there other girls whose grades were at issue?"

"Just sweet Melanie."

"Why do you think Miss Delacourt would do something like that?"

Sandra shook her head and a strand of wet hair clung to her cheek. She brushed at it impatiently. "You'll have to ask her."

"I take it you didn't ask?"

"I did not."

"And you formed no opinion about why she would do this?"

"I'm not paid to have an opinion."

Sydney realized she was getting nowhere. "All right. Now . . . you said you've worked at Hilyer since you finished college."

"That's correct."

"So you must have known Melanie for four years."

"I had her in class for four years, yes. Whether I or anyone else *knew* Melanie is debatable."

"Why do you say that?"

"Miss Bryant, I may as well admit to you I didn't like Melanie Whitman."

It fell far short of being a shocking revelation, but Sydney tried to look at least a little surprised. "May I ask why not?"

"It was nothing specific, just instant antipathy. And it was mutual. She didn't care for me either. She made no secret of it."

"But she was only thirteen when she started here . . . what could you have found in a thirteen-year-old to make you dislike her on sight?"

The woman shrugged her shoulders. "It's been so long now I can't recall. But I'll tell you what I didn't like about her this past year."

Sydney had an inkling of what it might be. Jeff King had arrived this past year.

"Melanie dear thought she had the corner on being a woman. She was full of herself. Flouncing around, tossing that mane of blond hair—" Sandra touched her own hair absently "—and batting her eyelashes at . . . at . . ."

"The male teachers?" Sydney suggested.

"Mark and Jeff, yes, but also at every male who showed up on campus. The gardener, for heaven's sake. The other girls' fathers."

"I would think flirting might be common behavior, given the girls are isolated from men a good deal of the time, in particular the girls who live on campus."

"Well, yes, most of them flirt to some extent, but Melanie did more than just flirt."

"Oh?"

"She was sleeping around."

"How do you know this? I mean, you and she weren't on the best of terms."

"You hear talk. The shower room talk in an all-girl school would make men blush if they could hear it. These girls are not shrinking violets."

"What specifically did they say?"

"I'd prefer not to use that kind of language, but the gist of it was that she was working on breaking the Heinz record of fifty-seven varieties."

"She was involved with more than one man?"

Sandra laughed harshly. "Sometimes more than one man a night."

"This wasn't just talk?"

"I don't think so. But, of course, how could I know without following her around? And I have better things to do."

Sydney imagined Sandra Lockwood was more than willing to believe ill of Melanie. "May I ask if the talk ever referred to anyone by name?"

"There may have been a name or two mentioned, but I couldn't tell you who they were."

"But not Jeff King? Or Mark Anderson?"

That apparently struck a nerve; the woman's expression hardened. "I don't believe that Mark has it in him, to be frank."

"And Jeff King?"

"No."

"Really. I've heard that a number of the girls have crushes on Mr. King."

"I'm sure they do."

"Melanie wasn't one of them?"

"She may have had a crush on him. I don't know. I'm reasonably sure Jeff wasn't interested in her."

"Have you ever discussed her with him?"

Sandra's eyes narrowed slightly. "Only since her death. Believe it or not, Miss Bryant, after being around teenage girls five days a week, the last thing I want to do is talk about them on my time off."

"Do you and Jeff King see each other on your time off?"

"See each other?" She chewed at her bottom lip before answering. "I don't think you could call it that. We've had dinner a few times after a rough day at school, that sort of thing."

"What I'm getting at is whether you would have known if he and Melanie had been involved."

"I would have known."

Sydney regarded her with interest. "You sound quite sure about that; but having only had a few dinners with him, it doesn't seem to me as though you could be *that sure*."

"I am. Remember, we've worked together for these past nine months."

"But not closely. I seem to recall the physical education facilities aren't anywhere near the building where he held classes. So you weren't passing each other in the halls. I assume you both had full schedules?"

"Lillian doesn't believe in free periods for the teachers. But Jeff and I saw each other in the morning before classes began, and frequently at lunch if he wasn't tied up in the lab. And, of course, after school in the teacher's lounge."

"Still, that would be at most an hour or so each day?"

"I . . . yes, I suppose it would," she admitted grudgingly. "But—"

"You've known Mark Anderson longer than you've known Jeff King," she said.

The change of tack apparently threw Sandra Lockwood. She took a full minute to respond. "Well, yes. He's been at Hilyer for . . . a number of years."

Clearly, his arrival at the school had not impressed her in the way Jeff King's had. "Did he ever discuss Melanie with you?"

"Mark?"

"Yes."

"I don't think so . . ."

"Were you aware that Melanie was a favorite student of his?"

"I can't say that I was, not until Nicole mentioned it yesterday."

"So, although you've known him longer than you've known Jeff—for a number of years, didn't you say?—you and Mark did not share confidences?"

"No, we didn't."

"No dinners after school?"

"Oh, maybe once or twice, in a group, if you know what I mean."

She knew. "May I ask how you came to the conclusion that Mark would not be interested in Melanie? Or she interested in him? You did say that, didn't you?"

"Well, yes. I did." She frowned and rubbed at the line which appeared between her eyebrows. "You've talked to Mark already, haven't you?"

"This morning."

"I don't mean to be unkind, but you only have to look at him to know he's not the type women fall for. Even foolish young women."

She was probably right, Sydney thought with a twinge of sadness.

"As for whether he was interested in Melanie, I suppose it's possible. Not likely, but possible."

Sydney glanced at the recorder to see if the tape needed to be changed. It didn't. She sensed Sandra Lockwood was watching her with a certain wariness, but when she looked back there was a smile on the woman's face.

"Just a few more questions," Sydney said, and smiled in return.

"Of course."

"Do you know why anyone would want to kill Melanie Whitman?"

"No, I don't," she said smoothly.

"Do you know what Melanie was doing Thursday night before she was killed?"

"No."

"When was the last time you saw her?"

"That day in class, second period."

"How did she seem to you? Did she seem nervous or upset about anything?"

"I don't remember that she was nervous. She didn't participate in class, though. She didn't even dress for gym."

"Why?"

"I can't answer that. She had some kind of an appointment that morning at nine-thirty. She was present when I took roll call, and after she came up to me with a note from Lillian excusing her from class."

"The note didn't indicate what kind of an appointment she had?"

"No. It's a printed form. There's a place for the student's name and a place to put the time that the pass is good for. There are boxes to check which indicate the reason the student is being excused. Hers was checked next to 'appointment.' And, of course, there's a place for the authorized signature, in this case Lillian's."

"Melanie didn't—"

"She wouldn't have told me, Miss Bryant. Even if I had asked."

"She didn't say anything to you at all?"

Sandra Lockwood started to shake her head, but she blinked and looked at Sydney in surprise. "Now that you mention it, she did, but I don't think it will be of any help to you.

"What did she say?"

"I was watching the other girls warm-up for tennis. She came up to me, handed me the note and said, 'It's thirty-love.' "

"Thirty-love?"

Lockwood smiled archly. "She was telling me the score."

CHAPTER TWENTY-FIVE

It took nearly an hour to get back to University City from Old Town. A car had overturned on Interstate 5. Although the accident occurred in the south-bound lane and she was heading north, traffic was inching along in both directions.

Stuck driving at five miles an hour or less, Sydney was forced to turn off the air conditioning to keep from overheating the engine. By the time she made the turnoff onto San Clemente Canyon Road, she was drenching wet.

The apartment was cool and dark from the shades she'd had installed the summer before. It was also silent. Nicole apparently was still at the show.

Sydney locked the door and headed for the bathroom to take a shower, kicking off her shoes and unbuttoning her blouse along the way.

The phone rang. She looked at it with a frown. It might be her mother, or Nicole needing a ride home, or Ethan, or even Mitch.

Should she answer? What with the heat, humidity, and having inhaled about a ton of car exhaust fumes, she wasn't in the mood to talk to anyone.

Any of the most likely callers would need to be handled with care—her mother, because she was her mother; Nicole, because she'd been through a lot; Ethan, because she had a guilty conscience about Mitch; and Mitch, because of Ethan—and she wasn't up to caring right now.

All she wanted was a lukewarm shower, and she was damned well going to have it.

It seemed to her that she could hear the phone still ringing as she showered, but when she turned the water off and listened, there was no sound.

"Good," she said, and turned both faucets back on. The first blast of water from the showerhead was icy, causing her to gasp. The cold raised goose bumps on her skin.

She closed her eyes and leaned her head back so the water sprayed her face. When she could no longer hold her breath, she stepped back.

The nice thing about lukewarm showers, she thought as she reached for the soap, was that she didn't have to worry about the hot water running out.

The water had lowered her body temperature enough that when she finally got out of the shower, it felt good to wrap a towel around herself. She used a second towel to cover her hair, then walked into the bedroom.

In the dim light, she nearly tripped over Nicole's backpack which Nicole had left on the floor by the bed. She gave it a nudge with her foot, pushing it under the bed, and continued to the closet to get something clean and cool to wear.

She dropped the towel, stepped into a pair of cotton panties, and her oldest, most comfortable jeans. Hundreds of washings had faded them to near-white, and the fabric was incredibly soft.

As she fastened the snap at the waist, she heard the bedroom door swing open behind her.

Nicole, she thought, and half turned.

But it was Ethan who was standing there.

For a moment, neither of them moved. Their eyes held, but in the darkness she couldn't read his expression. She reached up and unwrapped the towel from her hair, using it to cover her breasts.

"Sorry," he said. "I didn't think you were home."

"What are you doing here?"

"I misplaced the key to my mother's house."

"Oh." She had extra keys to the Ross house hanging on a rack inside one of the kitchen cupboards. She often watered the plants at both houses when their mothers were away.

Ethan smiled faintly. "Obviously, I didn't lose the key to your place."

"No."

They fell silent. She stood on one foot, using the other to wipe at a trickle of water which ran down the inside of her calf.

"Did you get a key?"

He held up what she supposed was the key for inspection. "I tried to call, but you must have been in the shower."

"Hmm. Probably. Are you going by the house?"

Ethan nodded. "I'm supposed to leave the key under a flowerpot so the plumber can get in and have another crack at fixing the bathroom sink."

Sydney was acquainted with the sink in question. On occasion, for no discernible reason, it shot water straight up in the air. "He's a brave man."

"Yes."

Water dripped from her wet hair onto her bare back. "Well," she said. "Maybe I should get dressed?"

"Sydney . . . do you know that I—"

"Hello!" a voice called from the other room. "Anybody here?"

"Nicole's home," Sydney said. She held the towel closer. It felt good against her skin, and she realized that she was probably blushing.

Ethan backed out of the doorway and pulled the door closed.

CHAPTER TWENTY-SIX

Sydney found Nicole and Ethan in the kitchen, sitting side by side on the kitchen table, and companionably using their fingers to eat cold sweet-and-sour pork from the carton.

"This is *so* good," Nicole said. "And I'm starving."

"Didn't you have lunch?"

"I thought I'd get something at the theater, but I wasn't about to pay a dollar and a half for a week-old hot dog on a month-old bun."

Sydney had eaten a few hotdogs at the show and didn't think they were that bad, but she only smiled and shook her head. She opened the refrigerator to see what else there was to eat.

"And the nachos. Ha! They shouldn't be allowed to even call them that. That cheese stuff should be used to fill the potholes in the road."

Ethan laughed, nearly choking in the process.

Nicole tried to keep a straight face, but a smile played at the corners of her mouth. "And that so-called butter flavoring they put on the popcorn . . . be real. I mean, that stuff has got to clog an artery or two.''

"I think I just lost my appetite," Sydney said, and closed the refrigerator door.

"Have some of this." Ethan held out a piece of pineapple to her.

It didn't look particularly appetizing, but she ate it anyway. "Not bad."

Ethan nudged Nicole. "You see, I have her eating out of my hands."

Sydney made a face at him. "Watch out, I bite."

"I can hardly wait."

Nicole's eyes widened as she looked at Sydney. "Uh, I think I'll try to study for awhile before the girls come over."

"I thought you were starving?"

"This'll do," Nicole said, taking the carton from Ethan's hands and slipping off the table. "See you guys later."

They watched her disappear through the door.

"I think she thinks we want to be alone," Ethan said.

Sydney leaned against the kitchen counter. "Well, we're alone, all right."

"How was your date last night?"

"It wasn't exactly a date."

When Ethan had been sixteen and she was eight, he'd learned to arch a single eyebrow. It had driven her crazy then—because she couldn't do it no matter how hard she tried—and it drove her crazy now.

"It wasn't a date," she repeated. "I needed to talk

to him about Nicole's friend."

"He's running that case?"

"Supervising it." Officially, the case belonged to a homicide team which included a sergeant, three detectives and an evidence technician; but by taking an interest in it, Mitch had effective control.

"You didn't mention that the other day."

"Didn't I?"

"No."

"I guess I didn't want you to get the wrong idea."

His eyebrow arched again.

"Don't do that," she said.

"Do what?"

"You know what." She raised both her eyebrows. "We talked about the case. He told me some very interesting things."

"Like what?"

Sydney told him, briefly, what Mitch had told her the night before.

"Not much there," Ethan noted. "To go on, I mean."

She inclined her head in agreement. "Mitch says they're getting nowhere on it."

"What about you?"

"About the same. I talked to two of Melanie's teachers and got completely conflicting stories about her."

"That's not unusual. When I was a cop, I'd hear a different story from everyone involved in whatever I was working on. It got to be I was suspicious if any of the stories sounded too much alike."

"Police paranoia," she said, and laughed. One of the side effects of being a cop was to distrust anyone who wasn't a cop. In those days, Ethan had been every bit as paranoid as the rest of them.

He'd looked awfully good in his uniform, though.

She smiled, remembering.

"What?"

"Nothing. As I was saying, I don't have a lot of answers so far, but I'm hoping that Terri Allison might be able to provide a clue."

"The police have already talked to her, haven't they? Mitch would have told you, I assume, if she'd said anything significant."

"That *they* thought was significant."

"You think they'd miss something?" His expression was skeptical.

He might not be a cop any longer, and he didn't pretend to trust Mitch, but she thought a part of him still wanted to believe the good guys didn't make mistakes.

"I have a few advantages over the police," she said. She counted them out on her fingers: "One, people don't always tell the police everything they know; two, Nicole and her friends will say things to me they'd never say to a male cop; and three, I can remember being their age. None of those cops was ever a teenage girl."

"I hope not."

"Chauvinist."

"I don't think the department would approve of cross-dressing. But anyway, how is having been a

174

teenage girl going to help you?"

"I can think the way they do."

"Now there's a scary thought."

"Hush, Nicole will hear you."

"Nicole and I are friends. She knows I don't mean her. But how do they think?"

"Inversely."

"Well, that I believe, but I still don't see the point."

"The point is, sometimes they believe they can make other people believe the opposite of the truth by actually telling the truth."

"You've lost me."

She sighed. "You know the way men brag—"

"Some of them," he amended.

"Right. Well, no one believes them because they're usually lying."

"Now that's a sexist argument if ever I've heard one."

"Girls, on the other hand—or some of them—know if they tell the truth in a flippant enough manner, adults will assume they're being sarcastic and are lying."

"Huh. That sounds a lot like the reasoning of a criminal mind."

"The juvenile mind."

"Which leads us to?"

"According to what the police have been told, Melanie wasn't known to be dating anyone, but I wonder if she might have, at least once, let it slip." She paused. "If she was involved with one of the teachers, for instance, she might have said, 'Oh

175

yeah, Mr. King and I are going out on his boat to you-know-what our brains out.'?"

"'You-know-what'?"

"You know. Anyway, it might be the truth—"

"This King is the good-looking one?"

"Right. It might actually be the truth, but by saying it in that way, Melanie would assume no one would believe her."

"I don't know . . ."

"The p.e. teacher told me that the girls could get pretty crude in the locker room. She also said in the last year or so Melanie had gotten a reputation. That she was getting around."

"So?"

"It could all have been a smoke screen. Pretend to be with a different guy every night, while the truth was she was involved with someone."

Ethan frowned. "I don't know," he said again. "I think you may be reaching here."

"Maybe so. But I have nothing to lose."

He looked at her curiously. "What's interesting to me is wondering what was in your twisted little mind while you were in high school. What devious plan did you come up with then that made you think of this now?"

"I'll never tell."

"Hmm. I think I should talk to Nicole. If you understand her so well, maybe she understands you."

"I don't even understand me sometimes," she said, and felt herself begin to blush. That damned kiss.

"After you left last night with Mitch, she kept

watching me as though she thought I might spontaneously combust."

"She thinks you and Mitch are fighting over me."

"I wouldn't fight Mitch," he said with a smile, "but I might shoot him."

CHAPTER TWENTY-SEVEN

The girls arrived an hour later—there were three —and brought enough pizza with them to feed a football team.

Nicole, who'd finished off a carton of cashew chicken and two huge egg rolls after Ethan left, took one of the boxes and sat down on the floor with it on her lap. "I'm famished," she said.

Sydney shook her head in wonder.

"This is Terri," Nicole said, indicating a pretty red-haired girl who smiled at her wanly, "and that's Amber . . ."

Amber, wearing a Whitesnake T-shirt, flashed a high-voltage grin as if someone had thrown a switch, and just as quickly turned it off.

"And Velvet. That's her real name."

Velvet made a face. "My mother had a fabric fetish. My brother, Roy? His real name is Cordu-roy."

"It could be worse," Amber said as she selected a piece of pizza and began picking the mushrooms off it. "Polyester? Spandex?"

"Hey, watch out," Velvet said, "you're talking about my mother's future grandchildren."

"Guys," Nicole said, trying to finish her introductions, "this is Sydney."

A chorus of hellos followed, and they settled down to eat.

Velvet, a heavyset girl who covered her mouth when she smiled, was the only one not eating. She sat with her hands folded primly in her lap while the others dug in.

Sydney sat on the couch next to Terri. "How are you doing, Terri?"

"Not great, but I guess I'll live," she said, and frowned. "I keep doing that."

Nicole looked at her with sympathy. "Me too. I say something like, 'The heat is killing me', and what I just said suddenly hits me."

"Don't worry about it," Sydney said. "No one thinks you're making light of the situation."

"It's sort of strange how many words we use without meaning to. Without thinking about what they really mean." Nicole licked at the tomato sauce on her fingers. "And to try not to . . . it isn't easy."

"No, it isn't." Terri put her piece of pizza down and looked at Sydney. "Nicole said you're trying to find out who killed Melanie. You're a private investigator?"

"Yes. I wanted to talk to you about what happened that evening. When you last saw Melanie." She'd spoken softly, to Terri alone, but found that she had everyone's undivided attention.

"I already told the police everything I know. I don't think it helped them."

"I know it must be hard for you to talk about it, but I'd really appreciate it if you would tell me what you told them."

"Go on," Nicole urged.

Terri looked at Nicole, and then at Velvet and Amber who nodded their agreement. "All right, but it really isn't much."

Sydney considered turning on the microcassette recorder, but decided against it. She didn't want to make it any more difficult for Terri than it already was.

"Melanie and Nicole and I were at the library," she said. "Studying for our chemistry final. They were helping me because that stuff is sort of over my head. I don't know why I even signed up for it."

Velvet extended a sandaled foot, touching Terri's knee with her toes. "I know."

"Oh, all right. I signed up for chemistry 'cause Jeff is so . . . so . . ."

"So," Amber said. Her eyes rolled heavenward. "He is, isn't he?"

"Anyway, I wasn't the only one. Maybe Nicole and Melanie would have been in that class anyway, but most of us were there to drool."

Amber nodded decisively. "Next year, I'm signing up for chemistry, biology, *and* math. Three hours!" She clasped her right hand over her heart. "Can one woman take it?"

"I don't know," Velvet said, "why don't you find a woman and ask her."

181

"Hey, you guys, this is serious." Nicole exchanged a sympathetic glance with Terri. "Just ignore them, Terri. Go on."

Terri nodded, but there was a look in her eyes that hadn't been there before. Sydney thought, on some level at least, the girl was enjoying being the center of attention.

"Where was I?" she asked. "Oh, that's right. We were studying for the chemistry final. We were in the library at one of the tables, going over Melanie's notes. She takes . . . I mean, she took great notes. I think Nicole was getting it, but I was like, in the dark."

"When did you guys leave?" Nicole asked. "I never even knew you were gone."

"Seven? I think it was seven."

Sydney interrupted, "You're not sure of that?"

"I'm pretty sure. Nicole was—" Terri looked at Nicole "—like, oblivious, really into that stuff. Then Melanie said she had to see someone at seven-thirty and she'd better go."

"She didn't say who?"

"No. The way she said it, it was like, secret. I got the impression she wouldn't tell me, so I didn't ask. But . . . she said she had to go and since my brain cells were overloaded, I said I'd walk out with her." Terri paused. "We said goodbye to Nicole, but I don't think she even heard us."

"I didn't," Nicole said.

Sydney could tell it troubled Nicole that she'd missed her friends' goodbye. It was the kind of thing that could play at a person's mind: if I had done this instead of that, would things have turned

182

out different?

It was a question for which there would never be an answer.

"We left the library," Terri continued, "talked for maybe a minute or so on the walk out in front, and then I went my way and Melanie went hers."

Melanie's way being to her death, Sydney thought, and knew they all were thinking the same thing.

"What did you talk about before you separated?" she asked, only partly to distract them from grimmer thoughts. "Do you remember?"

Terri took a deep breath and held it, as though that would help her concentrate. Sydney was beginning to wonder if the girl would pass out from lack of oxygen when Terri let her breath out in a rush.

"She told me . . . she said not to worry about the chemistry final."

Amber and Velvet shared a disappointed look. "That's *all?*" Amber asked.

"Well, and she told me the trick to doing well in chemistry is to forget about the textbook and study the notes."

For a moment, no one spoke. Amber used her fingernails to free a piece of pepperoni from a mass of cheese. Nicole appeared lost in thought.

"Which direction did she go when she left you?"

"Hmm?"

"Did you see which way she went?"

"Oh. Towards the pool, I think. But I didn't look back to see."

Velvet's brown eyes widened. "If you had, you

might have seen him. The killer."

"I didn't see anyone. I'm sorry," she said, "I'm not much of a witness."

"Thank you," Sydney said, and patted Terri's hand. "The thing about investigating something like this is you never know what little detail may turn out to be important. The strangest bits and pieces of information can sometimes solve a case."

Terri brightened slightly. "I really liked Melanie. I would do anything to help find out who killed her."

"Me too," Velvet murmured.

"I have a few more questions, for all of you."

"Sure."

"About Melanie. Do you know whether she had a boyfriend?"

"The police asked me that. She never mentioned any special guy, but I don't know. We were friends, all of us, but I don't think any of us were really close to her. I mean—" Terri looked to the others "—we're all sophomores. She was, like, above us."

"But she didn't act that way," Velvet was quick to add. "She was always nice to me."

Terri nodded. "Always. But she never said anything to me about a boyfriend."

Sydney glanced at Velvet. "How about you?"

"No," Velvet said, shaking her head, "but there *must* have been somebody."

"Why do you say that?"

"You know." She couldn't quite hide her envy. "Melanie was so pretty."

Sydney realized belatedly that she'd never seen a photograph of Melanie Whitman. "Nicole, do you have a yearbook with her picture in it? Nicole?"

Nicole looked up blankly; apparently she'd been off in a world of her own. It was easy to see how Terri and Melanie had been able to leave without her knowing. "What?"

"I'd like to see a picture of Melanie. Do you have a yearbook?"

"Sure. In my room." She put the pizza box aside and rose gracefully from an indian-style position. "I'll get it."

"Oh, I want to go with you," said Amber, who got up with a little less grace. "You promised to show me the new computer your dad bought for you."

"That's another thing I don't get," Terri said, watching after them as they went out the door. "Computers. Nicole is so smart."

"She is," Velvet agreed. "It isn't fair. She's smart *and* pretty. I mean, look at this." She smiled widely, showing a gap between her teeth. "My mom says I look like Lauren Hutton when I smile, but I'd rather look like her in a bathing suit."

"Try having red hair."

"Yeah, that's bad," Velvet said with the brutal honesty of youth.

"About Melanie," Sydney said, trying to get them back on the subject. "You never heard her say anything about being interested in anyone?"

"Melanie didn't talk about guys to me," Velvet said, and looked at Terri. "I figured she maybe thought I'd never had a date and wouldn't know anything about them, which is true."

Terri shrugged. "All I can remember is once she

185

mentioned she really liked Tom Cruise, but I kind of doubt that's what you mean."

"No, not exactly."

"Sorry."

"In talking to people about Melanie these past two days, I was told that there was some gossip about her at the school." Sydney hesitated. "Someone suggested to me that Melanie was playing around."

The girls frowned at each other.

"Who told you that?"

"Someone who claimed to have overheard the talk."

"Whoever it was," Terri said heatedly, "is a damned liar."

Sydney knew she had to approach the next question carefully, or risk losing the rapport she'd built up with these girls.

"People lie to me sometimes, usually if they have something to hide." She gave that a moment to sink in. "The only way I have of finding out the truth, is by asking the questions raised by what I've already been told. Some of it isn't pleasant."

A little of the outrage faded from their faces.

"You were her friends. Maybe not her closest friends, but you went to classes with her, you studied together, you lived in the same dorm."

"Yes." The word was a whisper.

"You laughed together, maybe you cried together, and I know you'll miss her."

"Yes."

"What happened to Melanie was a terrible thing, and no one can ever bring her back, but you can help me see that no one hurts her anymore by telling lies about her.''

Velvet had raised her hands to cover her face, but Terri maintained eye contact. "Yes.''

"The police told me that Melanie spent her weekends off campus. She wasn't at home those days. I need to know where she was. And even if she was with somebody, if she *was* having an affair, that doesn't make her bad.''

There was movement at the door and Sydney realized that Nicole and Amber were standing there. She looked at each girl in turn.

"I need to know where she was,'' she said again. "And with whom.''

CHAPTER TWENTY-EIGHT

"There was a guy."

Sydney looked at Amber, surprised she was the one to answer. Then she realized Amber had been strangely silent when the others were talking about whether or not there was a man in Melanie's life.

"Do you know his name?"

"No." She sat back down on the floor. "But I know that she was in love."

The other girls were watching Amber intently, but she seemed unaware of them.

Nicole handed Sydney a thin black book with the words 'Hilyer Academy 1988' embossed in gold on the cover, then sat on the arm of the couch.

"Did she tell you that?" Sydney asked.

"Yes. She said she was very happy, and told me she was getting married the day after graduation."

Velvet let out a little yelp. "Married? You never told us that!"

"She asked me not to say anything."

"That's an awful big secret to keep, Amber," Sydney said carefully, not wanting to seem critical that the girl had kept her friend's confidence.

"I'd almost forgotten. I don't think she'd even have told me; but one day in gym she'd been excused early, and I went in for something. I forget what. She was coming out of the shower, and I saw she was wearing a ring on that necklace she always wore, with the—"

"A ring!"

Amber's smile made a reappearance. "You should have seen it, the diamond was *huge*."

"The guy must be rich," Velvet said.

"When was this?" Sydney asked.

"What? Oh, around Christmas."

"You kept this to yourself for six months?" Terri didn't try to hide her disbelief.

"I can keep a secret."

"You sure can," Velvet said. "You've kept it a secret that you can keep a secret."

Amber stuck her tongue out at them. "Anyway, she sort of told me that she was engaged, but no one else knew, and would I please not tell anyone. She never said another word about it."

"Have you talked to the police?" Sydney asked.

Amber shook her head. "They haven't gotten around to me yet."

Velvet glanced at Sydney and plopped down on the floor next to Amber, nudging her with an elbow. "I can't stand it in any longer. Didn't she give you any hints, like, who was this guy?"

"Well . . ."

"Tell us," Velvet urged.

190

"I don't know *who* he was, except he was older than she was, and he was crazy about her, and they were going to elope after she graduated."

"But she was only seventeen," Terri said. "How could she elope?"

"I don't know."

Sydney was less concerned with the logistics of elopement than with the man's identity. "Did she tell you where she met him?"

"No."

"But," Sydney persisted, "she was with him on those weekends?"

"I guess so. She must have been, if she wasn't at home."

"Every weekend?" Velvet asked.

Terri leaned forward. "She was with him. You mean, *with* him?"

"What Terri wants to know is," Nicole said, matter-of-factly, "were they having sex?"

Sydney looked at Nicole, a little surprised at the girl's directness; but she reminded herself that to be fifteen these days was to be surrounded by allusions to sex. No doubt she might have phrased it even more directly.

Amber glanced at Sydney and frowned, her color rising. "I guess they were. I didn't ask her that. I wouldn't ask anybody *that*."

"Do you know where they went?" Velvet looked a bit scandalized. Of the four of them, she was the naive one. "His place?"

Amber sighed. "I guess so. They sure weren't in her room at the dorm."

"Wow!"

The conversation turned to speculation about who else in school might be sexually active—Miss Delacourt's name among those they judged were not—and Sydney let her attention wander.

An older man.

The world was full of older men, but there were, of course, two who came immediately to mind.

If Melanie had been having an affair with Jeff King or Mark Anderson, it shouldn't be too difficult to confirm that fact. If it had been going on for awhile—since before Christmas, Amber had said—the chances were good someone, somewhere, had seen something.

It wouldn't take much effort to canvas both men's neighborhoods.

Sydney opened the yearbook and thumbed through the pages. She found Melanie Whitman's photograph without difficulty.

Hilyer Academy had gone back to the basics. Although the photographs were in color, the girls wore black sweaters accented with strands of pearls.

Melanie had indeed been pretty: high cheekbones, an aristocratic chin, a delicate nose. She'd worn her blond hair swept up for her senior picture, exposing the exquisite line of her neck.

Her blue eyes were her most compelling feature. The intelligence in them showed in the direct way she gazed into the camera.

She had signed her first name only across the right corner of the picture.

Melanie.

Sydney turned slowly through the pages until

she came to the candid photographs. There were several shots of Melanie, including one where she was standing next to Nicole. Both were laughing and pointing at something off camera.

There was also one with Melanie standing in front of the class, presumably reading from an open book she held in her hands.

Mark Anderson was also in that picture. Sitting at a desk to one side, and watching her with an adoring look on his face.

CHAPTER TWENTY-NINE

Sydney was restless.

Terri and the other girls had left shortly before nine, and Nicole had turned in soon afterwards. When she'd looked in on her, Nicole had been asleep, but even in her sleep the girl seemed troubled. Her mouth was drawn into a frown and once or twice, as Sydney stood there watching, Nicole had whimpered.

Bad dreams?

Sydney closed the bedroom door and wandered through the apartment.

She took her old electric typewriter out of the hall closet and lugged it into the kitchen where she could type without disturbing Nicole. But when she sat down to transcribe her notes from the day's interviews with Mark Anderson and Sandra Lockwood, she found she couldn't concentrate.

She kept hearing things that hadn't been said, and reading second meanings into what had been.

"Shit," she said, turned off the typewriter and got up to pace. But the need to be doing something would not be so easily satisfied.

Should she call Mitch?

She was, she knew, obligated to give him Amber's name and tell him what the girl had said. No doubt he'd pass it on to the detectives working the case, and they could arrange to take a statement from her.

Not that there was all that much to it. The police had already assumed Melanie had been involved with someone. This was merely confirmation.

Moreover, it was a good bet they had ideas about who the someone might be. They might not have come to the same conclusions she had—that Anderson and King were the most likely candidates—but neither would they have ruled either man out.

Right.

She went to the kitchen phone and after a moment's indecision punched out the number to Mitch's home, which she'd memorized but never before used.

For some reason, her heartbeat quickened.

It rang twice before he answered. "'Lo?"

"Mitch?"

"Yeah. Sydney?"

"I'm sorry to call you so late, but I have some information you might be interested in," she said before he could get the wrong idea.

"On Whitman?"

"Yes. I talked to several of her friends this

196

evening. One of them told me Melanie was not only seeing someone, she had an engagement ring and said she was going to be married after graduation.''

"Really? Graduation is what? Next week?"

"I imagine it is."

"That's interesting."

"I thought so. I was told she wore the ring on the chain around her neck."

"Well what do you know? Now we have a missing ring to consider. Maybe the fiancé changed his mind about marrying her and asked for his ring back. She refused, he tore it from her neck, and she fought with him for it. Then he takes his trusty baseball bat, which he happens to have with him, and knocks the shit out of her. Hmm. Did she happen to be a Padres fan?"

It was gallows humor—cynical and irreverent, endemic among policemen—but in spite of herself, she smiled. "I don't think so."

"Right. Who is? Well, the ring being gone might mean it was a robbery, but I don't buy it. Somebody was gunning for her."

"Somebody was," she agreed, and told him what Amber had said about the seven-thirty meeting, and also that the fiancé was supposed to have been an older man.

"That limits it," he said dryly. "What is 'older' to a seventeen year old?"

"Your guess is as good as mine." Sydney turned and leaned against the kitchen counter, her eyes moving to the tape recorder which sat on the table a few feet away. The tape reminded her of Mark Anderson. "Have you been able to come up with any names? For the guy?"

"No one solid."

Sydney took a deep breath. "What about the teachers at her school?"

"You mean Mighty Mouse and Superman?"

That startled a laugh from her. "Yes. I talked to Mark Anderson today."

"And?"

"I think he was very fond of Melanie."

"Huh. I wouldn't think he'd be her type, maybe not anyone's type."

"I think it's probably more complicated than that. Remember, this is a girl whose father essentially abandoned her. Someone comes along who outright adores her, lavishes her with affection. I don't know that she would be able to resist."

"Maybe not. But what about King?"

"What about him?"

"If you were seventeen and could pick either of them, who would you choose?"

"He might not have been interested in her, though."

"Unless he's gay, he was interested in her. And I doubt he's gay."

"You talked to him?"

"I read his statement. And I've seen him in his natural habitat, surrounded by females. He was very open when we talked to him, came right out and said the girls were pretty much after him all of the time."

"Including Melanie?"

"According to him, yes."

"Did he admit to anything?"

"The man's not crazy. If he admits to hitting the sheets with one of the students, he's out of there. Those girls are all minors. He was surrounded by a hundred potential counts of statutory rape."

"Ninety-nine."

"What?"

"Nothing. What did he say his relationship with Melanie was?"

"A dedicated teacher and a gifted student. She flirted with him, he'd wink at her in class, give her a thrill; but he said nothing ever came of it."

"Do you believe him?"

"No reason not to. Yet."

The 'yet' meant they were still looking at him, a thought that reassured her. "Another one of the teachers at Hilyer is rumored to have a thing for King."

"Not Anderson, I hope?"

"No. Sandra Lockwood. She's the phys. ed. teacher."

"Yeah, well, when it rains it pours. This guy is a veritable monsoon season."

"The reason I mention it is she's bad-mouthing Melanie. It could be King didn't always keep his hands to himself."

"And Lockwood was jealous?"

"That's my impression."

"So you think Lockwood saw the smoke, and where there's smoke . . ."

"Yes."

"I'll have someone look into it." He paused. "It could also be Melanie was too much competition and Lockwood wanted her out of the way. If she's a female jock, she might not be adverse to a little batting practice."

Sydney winced. "Could be, although that particular chain of events hadn't occurred to me. Anyway, I thought you should know what I found out."

"Thanks. Still . . . even knowing there's a fiance, we're running in circles."

"I suppose so. Listen, I'd better go. I'm talking to King in the morning."

"Sydney?"

"What?"

"Watch yourself."

The rain started coming down at about the time Sydney turned on the news. She kept the sound low to not wake Nicole, and went to sit at the foot of the sofabed so she could hear.

The news was pretty much what it always was: a couple of murders, a drug lab busted in the east county, a hit-and-run accident that left two people dead—one of them a child—and an elderly man with Alzheimer's disease had wandered away from his home.

Nothing tonight about Melanie.

Sydney picked up the yearbook and studied the girl's face.

"You kept too many secrets," she said.

Lightning flashed somewhere distant and a five count later the thunder rumbled by. Sydney got up to raise the shades and open the window just enough to let in the fresh smell of wet air.

On the television, the weatherman promised clear skies and the start of a cooling trend.

CHAPTER THIRTY

Sunday, June 12th

Nicole had her notes and books spread all over the kitchen table, and was studying quietly when Sydney got up at seven a.m.

"Good morning," Nicole said, looking up with a smile.

"It is morning," Sydney agreed. She got a glass from the cupboard and went to the refrigerator to pour a glass of milk. "I'll get back to you later on whether it's good or not."

"Oh, it's one of those days."

"It is." She hadn't gotten to sleep until nearly three, her mind racing with possibilities and unanswered questions. By three a.m., logic had given way to dark suspicion, and she was ready to believe they *all* had done it.

Hadn't she seen a movie that ended that way?

"I'd better tell you," Nicole said, "I ate the leftover pizza for breakfast."

"My God, Nicole." She moved the backpack off the chair and sat down. "Where do you put it?"

"I'm a growing girl."

"You must be." She put her elbows on the table and rested her chin in her hands. "How's the studying coming along?"

"All right." Nicole surveyed the open books and binders spread in front of her and nodded. "Another fifteen hours, and I'll have it made."

"Fifteen hours?" On taking a closer look at Nicole, Sydney noticed that her eyes were red. "How long have you been at it this morning?"

"Since five."

"You couldn't sleep either?"

"I keep having this dream," Nicole said, and frowned. "About Melanie. It wakes me up."

Sydney thought of watching as Nicole slept, and how the girl had whimpered. "A bad dream?"

"Very bad."

"Do you want to tell me about it?"

"I think I need to tell someone. Maybe then it'll go away."

"I'm listening."

"It's always the same. I dream I'm walking down the pathway at school, the way I did Thursday night. Only in the dream, Melanie is alive and she's walking ahead of me. I try to catch up to her, but I can't. It's dark out, and I'm scared, but I think if I can only run fast enough and catch up with Melanie, we can walk together and we'll both be all right."

Sydney put her hand over Nicole's, but said nothing.

"It seems like the path goes on forever, it keeps twisting and turning, and the trees are closing in. I'm running as fast as I can, and I can hear myself breathing. And then—" Nicole faltered and looked at Sydney with frightened eyes "—I catch up to her. I touch her shoulder and she turns around, and then she's gone, just gone, and someone touches *my* shoulder, and I turn, and it's coming at my face."

Sydney could see the shudder that passed through Nicole's body, and she half stood, leaning across the corner of the table to put her arms around the girl. "It's all right," she said. "It'll be all right."

"I know it's only a dream, but it's coming right at me, and I have to wake up."

"What is 'it'?"

"I can't really see it as much as feel it. I don't know what it is." Nicole pulled away so she could meet Sydney's eyes. There were tears in her own. "But I know if it hits me, it will kill me."

Sydney kneeled by the chair and held Nicole as she cried. "You poor kid," she said.

She'd read once that people could not dream their own deaths. There was some mechanism in the human brain which would not allow it. In a dream, if death became imminent, the dreamer was jolted from sleep, heart pounding, body tingling with fear.

Superstition held that anyone who didn't awaken from such a dream would actually die because death was so unspeakably traumatizing that the psyche could not go through it twice.

How must it be to be brought over and over to the brink of death?

Maybe waking at five wasn't such a bad thing.

Later, as she was dressing, Nicole came into the bedroom and sat on the bed.

"You're talking to Mr. King today?"

"Yes. Don't you call him Jeff?"

"Only when I'm in his class."

Sydney smiled at Nicole's reflection in the mirror. "I gather you're not among his legion of fans."

"No. I mean, he's very good-looking, and I think he's a good teacher; but I don't want to call him by his first name, and I *don't* want to go to bed with him."

Sydney blinked. "Has he . . ."

"He never says anything, but there've been a few times when I've had to stay after? And he sort of looks at me, like he knows what I'm thinking, but I swear I'm not thinking that at all."

"Tell me about these looks."

Nicole sighed. "It's not easy to explain. But he does it all the time."

"Has he ever done more than look?"

"At me? Not really. Maybe a couple of times he's come up to me, to see what I'm doing in class, or in the lab, and his arm might brush against mine, but it was nothing . . . intense."

"Hmm." Intense or not, Nicole was only fifteen. She didn't need that kind of attention from a teacher. "What about Melanie?"

"You mean, did he flirt with her? Sure, all the time."

Sydney turned to face her. "Nicole, what about Jeff King and Melanie?"

"I don't know . . . I've thought about it a lot since last night when everybody was talking about this guy Melanie was engaged to."

"But what do you think?"

Clearly, Nicole had been waiting to answer this question. "He's the one," she said without hesitation.

CHAPTER THIRTY-ONE

Jeff King lived in one of the condominium developments in University City that sought to capitalize on the name La Jolla. It was actually a good mile east of the beach town's outermost boundary, but reality seldom had much to do with a developer's plans.

Call it La Jolla and jack up the price.

Pseudo-La Jolla was cluttered with condos and apartments, most with red-tiled roofs to reflect the hacienda orientation of southern California. Except Spanish haciendas were seldom built so close together that the owner-slash-occupant could reach out the window and touch the building next door.

King's unit overlooked a diminutive pool where even at eight-thirty on a Sunday morning, devoted sun worshippers worked on their tans. Their stillness reminded Sydney of lizards basking in the desert heat.

Were they cold-blooded as well?

Sydney rang the bell. When no one answered after a couple of minutes, she knocked on the door.

"Coming," a voice said.

Evidently she'd woken him up. She checked her watch to see if she was early, but she was right on time. The Sunday paper was on the doorstep, and she reached down to pick it up.

The door opened and from her vantage point all she saw were his bare legs. He was dressed only in tennis shorts, and his hair was mussed from sleep.

"Hi," King said.

She straightened. "Mr. King."

"It's Jeff, I told you." He took the paper from her. "And you're Sydney. Come on in."

The front room was dominated by a huge sectional sofa which touched on three of the four walls. A wood shelf ran along the top of the sofa, over the cushions, and was home to a dozen or more thriving green plants.

Behind the plants, the walls were covered with mirrors. The room was filled with Jeff Kings.

He tossed the paper on the sofa. "Have a seat while I put on the coffee."

She did as invited, watching him—as he no doubt intended—when he left the room.

A prime specimen of the male animal. If his face was strikingly attractive, his body approached perfection. Not the overwrought and chiseled perfection of someone who had to work at it, but a kind of easy magnificence.

King was another one of those men, like Mitch, who evoked a physical response from women just by being in the same room.

No wonder he had so many mirrors.

Assorted sounds came from the kitchen, including an "ouch" which she suspected was supposed to prompt her to go to his aid. She didn't.

After a moment he returned, running a hand through his hair and yawning. "It'll be a few minutes." He grinned at her. "So, Sydney . . ."

"Jeff. I have a few questions for you."

"Of course."

She took out the recorder. "You don't mind, do you?"

"No. Oh, I meant to ask, how is Nicole? She's staying with you, isn't she?"

Sydney nodded as she hit the record button. "She's doing fine."

"You're neighbors, someone told me."

"That's right."

"Lucky Nicole. She gets a private eye for a neighbor and I get Murray the shoe salesman."

"There's a certain similarity, actually." She held his eyes. "It's all in the fit."

King laughed. "I can guarantee, you have nothing in common with a salesman."

But you do, she thought. "Nicole tells me you're very popular with the students."

"Oh? That's good to know. Sometimes I get so caught up in what I'm trying to teach, I wonder if anyone's really listening."

"I'm sure they are. Melanie was one of your better students, you said."

"Absolutely. A very bright girl. Working on a college level."

"When we talked on Friday, you said something

to the effect that she'd had a little trouble in chemistry this quarter?"

"Hmm. Yes."

"What was that about?"

He scratched at his head. "Well, you know, I'm not sure what was at the bottom of it, but she kind of spaced-out on the mid-term."

"When was that?"

"Six weeks ago? I'd have to look at a syllabus if you want the date."

"It's probably not important. When you say spaced-out, what do you mean?"

"Just that. She was late to class, the last one in. And she sat there, staring at the test, and didn't answer a single question."

"That's curious. Did you ask her about it?"

"She told me her mind just went blank." He made a rueful face. "It happened to me once in college, on a biochem. test. I'd studied so hard, and I *knew* the stuff, but I couldn't complete the circuit from my brain to my hand. I was paralyzed."

Sydney made a mental note to ask Nicole what she knew, if anything. "But otherwise, she was doing well in your class."

"Very well." His smile was engaging. "The kind of a student that teachers want in their classes. Someone like Melanie can spark an entire class with enthusiasm. Nicole's that way, too."

"Nicole works at it. Right this minute she's studying for her finals."

"Glad to hear it."

"But back to Melanie. Did you have a personal relationship with her?"

"By personal you mean?"

"Did you ever see her outside of school?"

"Oh." He frowned. "It's entirely possible."

That was not the answer she'd expected. "Yes?"

"Sure. I took four or five girls to the zoo a couple of weeks ago. I don't think Melanie was one of them, but she might have been. I do that kind of thing all the time."

She regarded him for a moment, wondering if his candor was as self-serving as it seemed. "Actually, Jeff, what I'm getting at is, were you seeing Melanie Whitman."

"Seeing her? Romantically?"

"Yes."

Sydney had to admire the subtle change in his expression; one would have thought the idea had never occurred to him.

"No, of course not," he said.

"Some of the other students felt you flirted with her in class."

"Hell, I flirt with all of them. It's my nature."

"But nothing more?"

He looked amused. "Nothing more. They're little girls, Sydney. I prefer women."

"Not so little. And Melanie was beautiful."

"She was. But not beautiful enough to make me risk my job. Believe it or not, I can resist temptation when the price is too high."

Time to try another approach. "Do you mind if I ask you about Sandra Lockwood?"

"Sandy? What about her?"

"I've also heard talk that you and she were involved. When I talked to her yesterday, she told me you've gone out several times. Is that true?"

"We've gone out, but we're not—" he hesitated, turning his head as if listening for something. "The coffee's finished. You want a cup?"

"No, thanks."

"I'd better have one. I had too good of a time last night." He gave her a boys-will-be-boys grin and bounded off the couch. "Be right back."

He took his time in the kitchen, and Sydney idly glanced at the paper. A headline right at the fold caught her attention.

Girl Identified in Beating Death

She turned the paper over. Melanie's graduation photograph was in the lower left-hand corner. The caption beneath gave her full name.

The story's byline was Victor's.

So, the news was out. It was odd, she thought, that Victor hadn't called her—he liked to gloat—but when she scanned the first paragraph she saw Albert Whitman had finally been notified of his daughter's death. Griffith hadn't scooped anyone after all. The police had released the name.

"Sorry," Jeff King said, entering the room. "I had to wash a cup. Forgot to turn on the dishwasher last night."

Sydney indicated Melanie's photograph. "Did Melanie ever talk to you about her father?"

"Hmm?" He came over and picked up the paper, frowning. "The front page . . . Lillian will slip a cog. Excuse me, what was the question?"

"Did Melanie discuss her father with you?"

214

He shook his head and dropped the paper back on the couch. "Nope. We did talk about her mother once." He sat down and raised the coffee cup, but didn't drink from it. "She thought her mother copped-out by killing herself."

"Why was that?"

"She said if it had been her, and the son of a bitch had run out that way, she'd have gone after him with a gun." King took a swallow of coffee, and looked at her over the rim of the cup. "I believed her."

Sydney felt a tingle of apprehension. What he'd said had the ring of absolute truth, and she wondered if Melanie had been the one with the bat.

"They say men are violent," he went on, "but women are just as bad. You were asking me about Sandy? Now there's a woman I wouldn't cross."

"Why not?"

"I did go out with her a few times, nothing serious, but one Friday night we went to the Rusty Pelican for a few drinks after school. I don't know if you've been there, but it can get pretty wild on Fridays. A real crowd scene. One little chicky comes up to me—Sandy had gone to the ladies room, I think—and she's putting some moves on."

Sydney could tell he was enjoying himself, talking about it.

"So she's standing about a quarter-inch away, she has one arm around me, and she's laughing about something I said that even *I* didn't hear with all the noise. And all of a sudden, *wham!* She's gone."

"Gone?"

"Sandy had come back, and I guess she was feeling territorial or something, because she hauled off and belted this girl right in the face. Knocked her on her ass." He tilted his head, remembering. "It was, if I recall, a very nice ass."

"That must have been quite a shock."

King laughed. "You're not kidding. The girl started to get up and come after Sandy, but I think the smoke cleared or whatever, and she saw the look on Sandy's face. She made herself scarce."

"Did she say anything to you?"

"Sandy? Not a word. She just ordered another drink. But nobody, and I mean nobody, flirted with me the rest of the night."

Sydney could understand why. "But she didn't really have cause to do that, did she? Your relationship with her wasn't . . . intimate?"

"I don't kiss—or anything else—and tell," he said, and smiled lazily. He stretched his arms out along the back of the couch. "Next question."

"Thursday. Melanie was in class, I presume."

"Oh yes. Always in class."

"How did she seem to you that day?"

"You would ask. The girls were finishing up their lab assignments and turning in their equipment. I was so busy, I don't think I said more than two words to anyone the entire period."

"Did you see her at any time after class?"

"I'm sure I saw her in the halls, but I didn't talk to her."

"What period was this?"

"Fourth. After lunch."

"Was she on time to class?" she asked, thinking

about the appointment Melanie had had during second period.

"Well, I was late to class myself, so I can't really say who might have been tardy."

"Why were you late?"

He rubbed at the side of his nose. "I had a little accident in my biology class. Somebody let the frogs loose. They do it every year from what I'm told. A Hilyer tradition."

"Uh huh."

"So I was chasing these frogs down the hall."

"Right." She shook her head to clear the image that came to mind: King with the frogs, and not a prince among them. "So, Melanie was in her fourth period class and you saw her afterwards, but didn't speak to her."

"You got it."

"What time did you leave the campus?"

"Four-thirty. You can check with Miss Fair-weather, by the way. She practically creamed my car with that old clunker of hers."

"I thought she lived on campus?"

"She was running an errand for Lillian. On school time, but who's counting?"

"How did you spend the evening?"

"Ah!" He grinned and leaned forward. "At last we come to it. My alibi."

"You have one, then."

"But I don't. I was home, by myself, working on the final exam."

"All evening?"

"All evening. I had to finish writing the test so I could turn it in to be dittoed on Friday morning."

"Did you finish it?"

"Yes, and without a minute to spare."

"No one called or came by who could verify you were home?"

"The police asked me that, and I came up empty. No one called, I'm sure of that, but I must have waved hello to a neighbor or something. Whether anyone would remember it, I haven't got a clue."

"I see."

"That leaves me in the running as a suspect, I suppose."

She noticed that he didn't look too concerned. "Right now, I think everyone's a suspect."

"Who do you think did it?"

It was shrewd of him to ask, she thought. "I haven't come to a definite conclusion on that."

"I have."

"Oh?"

"Amazing as it might seem, I think Anderson did it. And I'll tell you why."

"Please do."

"It's no secret that he was a little nuts about Melanie. I don't blame him really. As you said, she was a beautiful girl. A little young, but Mark *needs* a young one."

"Needs?"

"Let's face it, a guy like Mark would have trouble with a real woman. All he can hope for is one of his students to get a schoolgirl crush on him. And that happens all the time to male teachers, even to the Marks in this world."

Sydney remained silent, waiting for him to go on.

"Anyway, she gets a crush on him, probably as a freshman. The years go by and he thinks it's going to last forever. But Melanie kind of breaks free. She turns sixteen, daddy's guilt pays for a new car. All of a sudden she's not stuck at school and lo and behold, there are *men* out there."

Or, Sydney thought, a good-looking new teacher arrives at the school.

"So, Mark doesn't seem quite as appealing, now, and she finds something better. Hell, Miramar Naval Air Station is just down the road, maybe she met a young fly-boy. Or some three-piece-suit type catches her eye. Whatever, she finds better things to do with her time than listen to Mark read love poems."

He seemed to be waiting for her to agree with him, so she nodded slightly.

"But Mark has spent four years waiting for this girl to grow up. He's been a gentleman. He's kept control. He's resisted temptation. And Melanie finds someone who'll give her what he can't, and it's all over."

"Maybe so," Sydney said.

"Mark can't have her, he's waited all these years, and he just flipped out. Maybe he didn't mean to kill her, maybe he was begging for her to come back to him, and she laughed." King's eyes narrowed slightly. "Young girls can be cruel, you know. They're not all innocent. If she told him exactly what she was leaving him for . . ."

He left his thought unfinished, but Sydney could fill in the blanks.

219

CHAPTER THIRTY-TWO

"—finds something better. Hell, Miramar Naval Air Station is just down the road, maybe she met a young fly-boy. Or—"

Sydney reached over, hit the stop button on the tape recorder and pushed rewind. Usually she was a good typist, and she'd transcribed the other interviews without difficulty, but Jeff King's tape was taking twice as long as the others had.

Perhaps because she found what he'd said so disturbing. Or the more she learned about the case, the less clear all of it seemed.

Or maybe she just needed a break. She'd been at it for nearly two hours.

She got up from the desk and stretched, then rubbed the muscles in the small of her back. She crossed to the window and stood for a moment, looking through the venetian blinds, watching the traffic go by.

It was hard not to envy the people in those cars. Presumably they were not working on a Sunday afternoon which, as the weatherman had promised, had turned out to be cool and clear. Neither had they lost sleep for the past few nights because of a young girl's murder.

With a sigh, she turned back toward the desk.

She'd bought a newspaper at Luigi's to read the story Victor Griffith had written. The article held no surprises and nothing sensational, just a succinct retelling of the facts.

And just the facts.

Victor hadn't even referred to Melanie Whitman as a coed.

His style generally was not so restrained, but given the wealth and social prominence of Albert Whitman, that wasn't totally unexpected. The newspaper's editor had kept a firm grip on the boy's leash.

What *was* interesting was a brief sentence in the last paragraph mentioning Whitman would be flying in to attend his daughter's funeral, which apparently had been hastily scheduled for Monday afternoon.

Sydney planned to be at the funeral. She wanted to take a look at this man.

Daddy dearest?

When she finally had caught up on all of her paperwork, she assembled the interview transcripts and her notes into a case file. After another look at Victor's article, she clipped it out of the paper and added it to the file. She took out a fresh legal pad intending to write down the questions she had about the case, along with the most probable answers based on what she'd learned so far.

The problem was she had a terrible suspicion she wasn't even close to finding the answers. She'd spent two and a half days working on it, and she was getting nowhere.

Her offhand remark to Jeff King about what mattered to a detective being "the fit" had not been as facetious as it might have sounded. The trouble was not that nothing seemed to fit, but that everything did.

She wrote down:

Who Killed Melanie Whitman?

After a moment's reflection, she added the numbers one through four and listed the names alphabetically.

Anderson

King

Lockwood

Unknown

Staring at the names, she realized the list also reflected her own ranking of the suspects according to probability.

Mark Anderson, for the reasons King had suggested, and more. He'd grown up without love, and having found it, could he stand to lose it?

As everyone kept pointing out, a man like Mark could not expect to have many chances for a relationship. Women, for whatever reason, seemed to prefer the men who were bad for them.

Nice guys not only finished last, sometimes they never got started.

Listening to Mark's voice on the tape as he'd talked about Melanie, Sydney was convinced more than ever that he had indeed been in love with the girl. Had King—or someone else—stolen her away?

As for Jeff King, maybe he'd taken his flirtation with Melanie a step too far. Had he broken his rule of noninvolvement with students and become her lover? Offering her what Mark Anderson—who was perhaps too much of a gentleman—had not? Had he led her on with promises of marriage after graduation, only to break it off when the day of reckoning came too near?

The one thing King had told her that she absolutely believed was that Melanie would turn vindictive if scorned by a lover. She'd grown up with a father who spent his time running away from her, and a breakup could have pushed her over the edge.

King might have killed her to silence her, to protect his career.

And Sandra Lockwood, feeling territorial toward King, might have murdered Melanie in a jealous rage over their real or imagined affair. The clumsy lies she'd told about Melanie's promiscuity had probably been intended to divert attention away from King.

As for the actual commission of the crime, who knew the campus better than the teachers who worked there? Who better to have arranged a meeting place where no one was likely to come upon them?

And the weapon? Maybe Melanie *had* brought it

with her—as protection, or to use as a threat, or even with intent to kill—only to have it taken away and used against her. If that was the case, Melanie might have brought on her own murder.

The police called it a victim-precipitated crime.

Of course, it could have been an unknown. Someone might have wandered onto the school grounds and come across the girl as she waited under the trees.

Whether for the ring she wore around her neck or simply because she was in the wrong place at the wrong time, Melanie could have fallen victim to a purely random act of violence.

In which case, they might never know the truth about what happened.

CHAPTER THIRTY-THREE

Nicole was at the gate waiting for her when she got home at two.

"What's wrong?" Sydney asked. "Did you lock yourself out of the apartment?"

"No, no." Nicole hooked her thumb under the silver chain around her neck and pulled it free of her blouse to reveal two keys. "I got a call from the school. From Miss Delacourt."

"Oh?"

Nicole fell in step beside her. "Melanie's dad is here. He wants to talk to me."

"How do you feel about that?"

"Not good."

"Then don't do it." She wanted to talk to Whitman, but not at the expense of Nicole's peace of mind.

"Really? I don't have to?"

"Of course you don't." Sydney opened the front door and held it for Nicole.

"Miss Delacourt won't like me saying no. She

won't like it at all."

"I'm sure she'll get over it."

"I wish *I* was sure. It was sort of like an order. I don't suppose you'd call her for me, would you? And tell her?"

"An order?" Sydney smiled. "I'd love to."

In her absence, Nicole had moved into the front room to study, and the floor was dotted with books. Sydney picked her way across the room to the phone, itself covered by a copy of the periodic table.

"What's the number at the school?"

Nicole rattled it off. "You don't mind if I leave the room while you talk to her?"

"Do whatever you want." The line began to ring.

"Good," she said, "I'm hungry."

Sydney covered the receiver with her hand. "Your dad better get home soon," she called after Nicole, "I'm running out of—"

"Hilyer Academy," a voice said in her ear.

"Lillian Delacourt, please."

"Oh, I'm sorry, you just missed her. Perhaps you'd like to call back . . ."

Sydney recognized the voice as that of the dorm mother. "Miss Fairweather?"

"Why, yes. Who is this?"

"Sydney Bryant."

"Oh! The private detective?"

"Investigator," she said automatically. "If you have a minute, Miss Fairweather, I have a few questions I'd like to ask you."

"Ask me?"

Sydney could hear the uncertainty behind the woman's words, and didn't want to give her a chance to consider the consequences. Her impression of Theadora Fairweather was that the woman loved to talk, but Lillian Delacourt held her in rein.

Lillian was not there now.

"I imagine you knew Melanie fairly well," Sydney said smoothly, "after four years."

"Well, I . . . yes, I knew Melanie. She was a very sweet girl. It's terrible that she . . . oh my."

"Did you see Melanie on Thursday?"

"The night she was . . ."

"Yes."

"Oh my. Did I see Melanie? Well, I saw her that day, of course. She was in the office that morning, to get her pass—"

"To be excused from second period?"

"That's right." ·

"Do you recall what kind of an appointment she was going to?"

"She wasn't really *going* anywhere. The Reverend comes to the school for his counseling sessions with the students. He has a little office here."

"Counseling?" Sydney frowned. She'd almost forgotten about The Reverend Wolfgang Hauff. "Was she having a problem in her classes or—"

"I can't really say, Miss Bryant. I arrange for Reverend Hauff to come to the school when one of the girls needs to talk to him, but I never ask the . . . uh . . . nature of the problem."

Sydney rather suspected the old woman preferred it that way. The problems of this generation were unsettling to consider. "I understand. How about later that day? Did you see Melanie after classes were over?"

"Oh my." The tremulous tone was back in her voice. "It was such a strange day . . ."

"Strange how?"

"Well, of course Jeffrey was chasing those frogs—I wish the girls wouldn't keep doing that—and I'm almost sure Melanie was there."

"The frogs," Sydney said.

"Last year one of the poor things got out and made it out to the road. A frog, I mean, not one of the girls. Well, naturally someone ran over it. All summer long the girls were telling dead frog jokes. Dreadful things—the jokes, I mean—and anyone who wore green was subject to all kinds of unpleasant remarks."

"About Thursday?"

"Was I rambling? Lillian says I ramble."

"You're doing fine. You don't remember seeing Melanie any time that evening?"

"No. Of course, I was in and out. I had some errands to run and, well . . . that's not important. I didn't see Melanie."

"I spoke to Jeff King this morning and he says you can verify that he left the campus at four-thirty."

"That's right, he did. That little car of his, I can hardly see it in my rearview mirror. They shouldn't make cars you can't see . . ."

Sydney straightened. How had she forgotten about Melanie's car? "Miss Fairweather, is there a place on the school grounds where the students who live on campus and have their own cars can park them?"

"Not many of them have cars. These girls are from well-to-do families, but we . . . that is, Lillian . . . advises the parents against it."

"Why is that?"

"Oh, the trouble they get into! They think nothing of driving down to Mexico, where the college students like to . . . party? We've had more than a few girls come back, sick from drinking and heaven knows what else."

"But Melanie owned a car."

"She did, and Lillian wasn't happy about it; but, of course, Mr. Whitman gives the school a generous endowment in addition to the tuition he pays."

"I see. Where did Melanie keep her car?"

"I think . . . there's a few spaces out behind the library. Adriane—Miss Shanfield, she's the librarian—parks there so she doesn't have to walk so far. Maybe it's there."

The police might have impounded the car, but Sydney thought not. There'd been nothing to indicate that the car was at all involved. She would have to take a look when she drove Nicole to school in the morning.

"Or maybe," Miss Fairweather was saying, "it's not."

"Back to Thursday. What about Mr. Anderson? What time did he leave?" Sydney hadn't asked that question of him, but no doubt the police had.

"Mark? I don't recall . . . but he was in with Lillian that afternoon. You might talk to her."

Something else to look forward to, she thought. "And Miss Lockwood?"

"Now, that is something I do know. She gives private lessons on Mondays and Thursdays to several of the girls who she feels have potential."

"Tennis lessons?"

"Yes. She's an excellent player. I believe she almost turned pro."

"And the private lessons would last until when?"

"Usually, from five to eight."

That was interesting. "Are you and Miss Delacourt the only members of the staff who live on the campus?"

"Yes. Well, there's the cook."

"What about the other teachers? Would any of them still have been on the school grounds between seven and eight that night?"

"There's only one other full-time teacher. Rachel Dillon teaches history and geography, but she was feeling ill as I recall." Miss Fairweather lowered her voice. "The change, you know. She left at noon."

"You said full-time. There are part-time teachers?"

"When we can get them. It's not easy to find teachers these days. Young people just don't think of teaching as a career the way they once did, and it's a shame. When I was a girl, it was what women did if they had to work. We were lucky to get Jeffrey . . . science teachers are so scarce. I honestly don't know what we would have done if Lillian hadn't found him."

"Were the—"

"I'm rambling again, aren't I? You asked about the part-time teachers. Well, the French teacher was here, but she was a substitute, and I don't think the poor dear knew what hit her. The last week of classes . . . the girls can get a little rowdy. Did I mention the frogs?"

"You did," Sydney said, and smiled. "Thank you, Miss Fairweather, for your time."

"Shall I ask Lillian to return your call?"

"That's all right. I'll be in touch."

CHAPTER THIRTY-FOUR

"You're off the hook for now," Sydney said, coming into the kitchen. "Miss Delacourt is out."

Nicole's hand stopped midway to her mouth, her sandwich momentarily forgotten. "Out?"

"Out. As in, she's not at the school."

"Oh, no! What if she's coming here?"

The stricken look on Nicole's face was almost comical, but Sydney regarded her seriously. "She wouldn't do that, would she? Show up without notice?"

"With Miss Delacourt, anything is possible. I don't know what she'd do. What if she's bringing Mr. Whitman to see me?"

"Nicole, you don't have to talk to her or anyone else if you don't want to. And if they *do* show up, I'll send them away."

"But she'll know I was here and didn't want to talk to her. Then tomorrow . . . tomorrow when I have to go to school . . . my life is over."

"Listen, don't worry—"

"If I didn't have to study, I'd go to another movie or something. But I've got to stay, I'm not even halfway through my notes."

"Nicole."

"And are you even going to *be* here for the rest of the afternoon?"

Sydney hesitated. She'd found Rachel Dillon's phone number listed in the directory, and had planned to call to request an appointment. With finals starting tomorrow, she might not have a better opportunity to talk to the teacher than today.

She also wanted to see if she could reach Reverend Hauff.

"Well . . ."

"Wait. I know what I can do. I'll take my stuff to my apartment. They won't look for me there. If you're gone too, they'll just think we had to go somewhere. Miss Fairweather will tell her you called, and I can say we *tried* to arrange a time, but we missed connections . . . it'll work, Sydney."

How—and when—had Nicole gotten so devious?

"I'm sure it will," Sydney said. "Though if Lillian Delacourt is quite the draconian overlord you seem to feel she is—"

"She is!"

"—she might be capable of finding you wherever you hide."

"I'll barricade the doors."

Sydney laughed. "I was teasing, Nicole. I'm sure she'd do no such thing."

"All the same, I'm taking my books and stuff to

236

my *own* room. I'll feel safer locked inside. My dad paid eighty bucks for that dead bolt. She'd never get past that."

Sydney hadn't the heart to tell Nicole there wasn't a lock made that couldn't be forced.

After she helped Nicole cart everything she needed to study to the Halpern apartment, Sydney called Rachel Dillon. Her luck was holding. The history teacher was home and quite willing to see her if she could come right over.

Reverend Hauff's number was also listed in the directory, and his housekeeper answered. The Reverend wasn't home, but the housekeeper gave her the address and phone number of the church he served and suggested that she try him there.

There was no answer at the church.

Sydney re-copied the number and address into her notebook. She'd call after she finished the Dillon interview, or maybe she'd just stop by the church on her way home.

She got a new cassette for her recorder, grabbed an apple to eat on the way over, double locked her own door and was off.

CHAPTER THIRTY-FIVE

Rachel Dillon lived in a post-World War II wood frame house on a tiny lot at the end of a shady street. Progress, in the form of apartment buildings or condominiums or corner convenience stores, had somehow missed this neighborhood. Driving down the street, it was easy to imagine how it had been in the 1940s.

Children playing in the street, old Buicks and Studebakers and Plymouths parked along the curb, neighbors talking over the backyard fence, the fragrance of fresh bread baking.

Sydney hadn't even been born then, and what she knew of that time came from watching old movies, but she felt a pull of nostalgia nonetheless.

Even now there was a quiet gentility about the place, in the well-kept homes, and in the rose bushes growing in almost every yard. These houses had porches, and porch swings, and a sense of permanence that was lacking in the one hundred and sixty thousand dollar houses they were building these days.

This neighborhood had character, an identity that hadn't been fostered by the builder trying to establish a sense of community, but had grown instead out of the good will of the people who lived here.

Not 'The Colony' or 'The Point' but *home*, and she suspected that many of its residents had lived in these wonderful houses for forty-odd years.

It was sad, though, that there weren't any children playing here now. Sad, too, that there was a for sale sign in the window of Rachel Dillon's home.

The front door was open and she could see through the screen into the modestly furnished living room. There were boxes on the floor and sheets of newspaper to wrap the breakables in.

"Mrs. Dillon?" she called, and knocked on the door frame. "Hello?"

A woman in her fifties peeked around a corner from what was probably the kitchen. She was dressed in a floral print shirtwaist, and her dark hair was streaked with gray. Her smile lit up her round face. "Yes, come in. You're the one who phoned?"

"My name is Sydney Bryant, and as I mentioned when we spoke earlier, I'm conducting a private inquiry into Melanie Whitman's death."

"I know. Please have a seat. If you can find a place in all this mess, that is."

Sydney moved a stack of neatly folded doilies from a chair onto the table and sat down. "I know from talking to some of the staff at Hilyer that you left the school early on Thursday."

"That's right. I haven't been feeling all that well lately."

"I'm sorry to hear that."

Rachel Dillon smiled. "It's why I'm moving, really. My sister has a house up in Carmel. We're both alone now, and it'll be nice to have each other for company. And my married daughter is living in San Francisco. I'll be able to see her more often, I hope."

"Will you be retiring from teaching?"

"Oh, yes." She nodded vigorously. "I've had quite enough of it, thank you."

"Why is that?"

"I don't care to bash my head against the wall, Miss Bryant. And that is what teaching has come to, I'm sorry to say. Everyone blames the teachers for the rise in illiteracy and the decline in test scores. Test scores," she repeated scornfully. "They may be the undoing of us all . . . these children need to be taught how to *think*."

"Was Melanie in your class?"

Her expression softened. "I'm sorry. I do rave on occasion, although not, I hope, without provocation. Yes, I had Melanie in sixth period history."

"Is that the last class of the day?"

"Actually there are seven, but Melanie was a senior, and they usually carry a lighter load. I believe she was only taking six classes this quarter."

So far, Sydney had accounted for five of the six; history, chemistry, physical education, English and literature. It didn't sound like a light load to her. "How was she doing in history?"

"She was an A student." Rachel Dillon sighed. "A teacher's dream. If only there were more like her. Or—" she frowned "—if she were still with us."

"How long had you known her?"

"Since the day she arrived. I was her advisor in her freshman year."

"But not in later years?"

"No. She requested Mark Anderson."

"I understand she was a talented writer," Sydney said.

"Yes, well, Melanie was good at whatever she did. I think Mark may have persuaded her prematurely that that was where her talents lay."

"What do you mean?"

"Oh, only that if he hadn't tucked her under his wing so fast, she might have found something she liked to do better. When she started high school, she'd intended to take some university extension classes—some of the girls do, since a small school like Hilyer has a limited curriculum—but he talked her out of that."

"Why do you think he did that?"

Rachel Dillon pursed her lips, as though considering how much to say. "I think, and I may be wrong because he never came right out and said what his objections were, but I think he didn't want her in that environment."

"A university environment?"

"Yes. Perhaps he thought there would be too many distractions for a girl her age."

Distractions like young men? "I take it you

don't agree?"

"Absolutely not, It would have been good for her to stretch a bit. Heaven knows, Melanie didn't seem to mind, but I thought Mark was too protective. A bright girl like that should have been broadening her horizons, not limiting them."

"But she didn't mind, you say."

"She didn't appear to. Although from what I know about her upbringing and background, maybe it was to be expected. Mark was, after all, giving her an awful lot of attention. And she was starved for attention when she arrived at Hilyer."

"Tell me about that."

"It's odd, Miss Bryant, but I remember the first day I met Melanie. That isn't always true with a student. Of course, there'd been some interest in her among the staff since her father had donated a considerable amount of money to the school."

"Did you ever meet Albert Whitman?"

Rachel Dillon shook her head. "That was another thing that may have made her stick in my mind. I won't pretend Hilyer doesn't function sometimes as a rather expensive escape from parental responsibilities, but even the parents who feel that way usually show up before they enroll their daughters to have a look around."

"I can imagine they would."

"It's not reflected in my salary, but the tuition at Hilyer is frankly outrageous. Certainly too much money to spend without assuring oneself that there will be value received."

"Whitman is filthy rich," Sydney noted.

"A lot of the parents are. But they still come and

243

chat with the teachers, discuss the curriculum and college prospects, and otherwise pretend that they give a damn. Melanie was by no means the only student in her circumstances, but her father actually enrolled her over the phone. He had, I was told, been sent a two-page brochure, and based his decision on that.''

"Not exactly a doting father."

"Not a father at all. I never understood how a beautiful girl like Melanie could be the result of that man's rather stagnant genetic pool."

Sydney smiled. "Maybe all of his genes were recessive."

"I've never been one for gaming, but I'd wager you're right." She fingered the top button of her dress. "The first time I met Melanie, I thought we hadn't a chance of saving her."

"Saving her?".

"From herself. She was quiet, withdrawn, but she had a tension about her you could *feel*. Have you ever been near a high-voltage power line?"

Sydney nodded.

"Then you know what I mean. Melanie just kind of hummed with pent-up energy . . . I thought she was in danger of harming herself. Her mother killed herself, you know."

"Yes."

"She frightened me in a way. The first week of school, I went in every morning, dreading that when I got there I'd be told someone had found her hanging from a rafter. Or with her wrists slit. Or overdosed . . . like her mother."

"But she got past that."

"Oh, yes, she did. And that was Mark's doing. I didn't always approve of his methods, but I have no argument with the results."

Sydney leaned forward. "How did he help her if she was that close to losing control?"

"As I said, he spread his wings and took her in. She was in two of his classes, one following the other, both at the end of the day. Very early on, they had some kind of a breakthrough, and afterwards he stayed after school to be with her every single day. They would sit in that classroom for hours."

"He did this on his own?"

"Yes. It was the most amazing thing. I've never seen a teacher that devoted to helping a student. Mark Anderson saved that girl's life."

But had he saved her life, Sydney wondered, only to take it later?

"I couldn't have done it myself," Rachel Dillon continued. "I wouldn't have known how, to be quite honest with you. But his instincts where she was concerned were unerring."

"So it would seem."

"And, of course, with all that attention, Melanie settled down. She and Mark were spending a lot of time together, and she knew he was always there for her if she needed him. Being able to rely on someone that way was something she'd never had before."

"How were things this year?"

"Well, a lot of changes were taking place. Melanie was going to graduate soon. She'd been accepted at a number of the universities she'd applied to. I don't know whether she'd decided which one she wanted to attend. I imagine it was an emotional time for her, leaving Hilyer and the friends she'd made."

"And leaving Mark?"

"I'm sure that was the most difficult for her. And for him as well, although I expect they would have kept in touch."

"How did Melanie seem to you these past few weeks?"

Rachel Dillon frowned. "I was worried about her."

"Why is that?"

"She'd been acting rather odd. She always was high-strung, even during the best of times, but lately I thought I detected a hint of . . . I'm not sure how to explain it. Instability? Fragility? You know, when I heard Melanie was dead, my first thought was she had killed herself after all."

"Were you aware she had sought counseling with Reverend Hauff?"

"No. But that surprises me. I wouldn't have thought she would have taken her problems to anyone other than Mark."

Unless Mark *was* the problem. "She had an appointment with the Reverend that morning."

"Oh my. The poor girl. Even on the day she died, she wasn't happy."

They were silent for a moment. Sydney remembered that Mark Anderson had quoted Melanie as saying, 'There are no happy endings.'

There hadn't been, for her.

Rachel Dillon sighed. "I haven't told anyone

this, because I didn't think it was anyone's business except for Melanie's and Mark's, but I saw them once."

"Saw them?"

"Yes. It was one day after class, a few weeks ago. I don't remember why now, but I was looking for Mark. The lights were off in his classroom, so I don't know why I opened the door, but they were in there."

"Go on," Sydney prompted.

"They were kissing. And not—" she shook her head for emphasis "—a little kiss. I don't know why they didn't hear me. I must have stood there for a minute or more, I was so shocked!"

"What did you do?"

"I went away, of course. I closed the door as quietly as I could and tiptoed away."

CHAPTER THIRTY-SIX

Sydney pulled into the parking lot alongside the First Methodist Church. The Reverend Wolfgang Hauff had finished services hours ago—it was now nearly dinner time—but when she'd reached him by phone after leaving Rachel Dillon, he had agreed to wait for her.

His was the only other car in the lot.

She got out of the Mustang and walked toward the building. He had promised to leave one of the side doors open for her, and as she neared she saw that the closest of them was ajar.

A thick pamphlet of some kind had been folded and wedged under the door to keep it from closing. She bent down and removed it. The door swung shut of its own weight.

"Miss Bryant, is it?"

Startled, she glanced up.

Wolfgang Hauff was standing in the shadows of an interior doorway. Dressed in dark colors, he blended into his surroundings. Even his skin seemed a little gray. When she'd seen him Friday afternoon at Hilyer Academy, his manner was solemn, nearly grim. It was today, too.

"I'm sorry," he said, and his voice was easily as gloomy as his appearance. "I didn't mean to catch you unaware."

She forced a smile. "Thank you, Reverend Hauff, for seeing me this afternoon."

"I want to help in any way I can." He held his hand out to her. "I'll take that for you."

At first she wasn't sure what he was referring to, and then she realized it was the pamphlet. She handed it to him. When his fingers brushed hers, she had to repress a shiver; the man's flesh was deathly cold.

Sydney put that thought aside. "You said you'd already given a statement to the police?"

He inclined his head. "The police asked me to come in after morning services, which I did. I had only just got back when you called." He sighed. "It was disconcerting to find myself discussing a murder on the Lord's day, but I appreciate that the police are anxious to have the matter resolved. As we all are."

"Yes."

"Thankfully, I've never been involved in anything as tragic as this . . . unfortunate incident. And I hope never to be again. But you have questions for me?"

"My questions will be similar to theirs, I'm sure."

"Indeed. Why don't we talk in my office? It will be more comfortable there."

She followed him down a narrow hallway. The office was something of a surprise. She didn't know what she'd expected, but it might have been the office of a corporate vice president for IBM: clean lines, modern, and tastefully understated.

Reverend Hauff sat behind the desk. "So, shall we proceed?"

"Did you know Melanie Whitman well?"

"No, not well."

"But you had a counseling appointment with her that morning."

"Yes."

"Had you talked with her before?"

"Only once before."

"When?"

"Oh, I'd have to check my records to tell you precisely. But it was probably six weeks ago, or at the very most, two months."

"Am I correct in assuming, Reverend Hauff, that she requested counseling?"

"That is the way it works." What might have been a smile flitted across his lips; there was no warmth in it. "I'd have to be a mind reader to know she needed guidance otherwise, wouldn't I?"

On the contrary, Sydney thought, how could he not have known? From what she'd been told, Melanie's emotional state was common knowledge. Still, there was nothing to gain by challenging him.

"I thought perhaps one of her teachers had suggested you talk to her," she said instead.

"No."

"What was the nature of the problem she consulted you about?''

"Ah. Well, sad to say, Melanie had discovered she was pregnant.''

At some level, Sydney had known that was what he was going to say. But even though she'd anticipated the Reverend's revelation, it gave her a moment's pause. "She had an abortion.''

It was not a question—she hadn't been pregnant when she was killed or the autopsy would have mentioned it—but he apparently considered it one.

"Yes. Against my advice.''

"Did she tell you what her circumstances were? As far as the father was concerned?''

"Melanie told me a lot of things. One of the most unpleasant was that the father of her child was one of her teachers.''

"Did she—''

"Tell me his name? She didn't have to.''

"Oh?''

"Of course, it was Mr. Anderson.''

"Why do you say 'of course'?''

He looked at her reproachfully. "Their relationship was not the secret they thought it was.''

"But she didn't actually say to you, 'Mark is the baby's father'?''

"Not in so many words.'' He sighed again, heavily. "I have counseled many young women who found themselves in trouble. They often have a misguided sense of loyalty toward the men involved.''

"So, when she consulted you the first time, it was because she was pregnant.''

"Yes. We talked about how she should tell *him*, and what her choices were if he did not offer to do the right thing by her. She mentioned abortion. I suggested she have the baby and put it up for adoption. I know a lovely couple who would have been thrilled to take the child. Or keeping it, and raising it on her own. She wasn't without resources, at least."

"What was her response?"

"She wasn't interested in continuing the pregnancy unless the father married her."

"Did she tell you why?"

"There were several reasons, apparently. One of the more compelling reasons she mentioned was that she was illegitimate. She was adamant about not putting the child through what *she'd* been through."

Sydney frowned. "Since she went ahead and had the abortion, the implication is the father refused to marry her."

"That was my impression. But she didn't want to talk about it."

"What *did* she talk about on Thursday?"

Reverend Hauff didn't answer immediately. He stroked his chin as if deep in thought.

"Reverend?"

"I'm sorry, I was reflecting on something she said to me. Something I'd forgotten."

"What was that?"

"A puzzle, actually. As I said, she gave me all kinds of reasons why she should terminate the pregnancy. She was very upset, and I guess I thought I'd misunderstood what she said. But now

I distinctly recall her saying, 'I won't be pregnant on my wedding day.'"

"You're sure about that?"

"Yes."

"Did you ask her to explain?"

"It wasn't possible. She was hardly coherent. I doubt she even knew what she was saying. But—" Reverend Hauff began to nod "—I imagine it was a slip of the tongue. She probably meant to say graduation day."

"Could be."

"Regardless, you asked me about the second session we had . . ."

"Yes."

"It was a good deal more subdued. She was quite calm, actually, which I thought was a good sign, considering. She said she'd done a lot of thinking since we'd talked before and had come to a decision.

"About what?"

"Ethics, of all things. She told me she had read an article in the paper about a teacher up in Orange County who'd been molesting his students. He would have these kids over to his apartment, and give them marijuana, or perhaps it was cocaine, and would coerce them into having sexual relations with him."

Sydney vaguely remembered reading about it. "Was she suggesting a teacher at Hilyer—"

"Again, she didn't come right out and say what she meant, but she'd written a letter to the editor of the *Union*, which I gather may have gone into some detail."

"I see." Something else to muddy up the waters, Sydney thought. "Is that all?"

"More or less. I had no advice to give her, but I'm not sure she was asking for any."

"That was the last time you saw or spoke to her?"

"It was. However, I was deeply disturbed by what she'd said, to the extent that I broke one of my own rules about confidentiality—after all, there are young girls at risk, if what she said is true—and went to Miss Delacourt."

Sydney nodded thoughtfully. "What did she say?"

"Not to worry, she'd handle it. But that night . . ."

". . . Melanie was killed."

CHAPTER THIRTY-SEVEN

Lillian Delacourt did not looked pleased to see her.

"Miss Bryant?"

"I think it's time we had a talk." Sydney moved past her and into the office.

The headmistress hesitated for a moment, closed the door and turned to face her. "Theodora told me you called earlier. I'm sorry we missed connections."

Sydney smiled faintly. "Oh, so am I."

"Is this in regard to Nicole?"

"Actually, it isn't."

"I see. Melanie."

The woman was as sharp as a tack. "Miss Delacourt, I don't know what you've told the police thus far, but I have a very strong suspicion it hasn't been, as they say, the truth, the whole truth, and nothing but the truth."

"Really?"

"Really."

"Well," Lillian Delacourt said, "if so, that would be of concern to the police, and not to you." At the desk, she picked up a small stack of papers and began to glance through them, as though the matter was closed.

"But it is my concern," Sydney said. "And I think the board of directors of this school might be concerned as well."

She looked up, her expression one of annoyance. "Is that a threat of some sort?"

"Take it in whatever way you want. You should know, as a licensed private investigator, I'm required to give the police any information I uncover regarding a crime."

"And exactly what is it, Miss Bryant, you think you have uncovered?"

"Melanie was murdered on this campus—"

"Oh, now there's a news bulletin." Lillian Delacourt smiled archly. "You *are* good."

Sydney refused to be baited. "She was murdered on this campus by one of her teachers, with whom she'd been having an affair."

"Oh? How is it that you've found this out and the police have not?"

"I said I shared information with the police, Miss Delacourt. They don't always share information with me, but we've been talking to the same people, and they'll probably come to the same conclusion."

"Well, I guess I'd better start looking for a new teacher for next fall. Who is it? Mark or Jeff? And please don't tell me it was Sandra or Rachel. I don't think of myself as a prude, but I find that—

orientation, shall we say?—extremely distasteful."

"You are responsible, not only for the education of these girls, but also for their emotional and physical well-being. Melanie and Mark Anderson—"

"Mark?" She made a clicking sound with her tongue. "I would have thought Jeff. Well, at least it'll be easier to replace Mark. Science teachers are almost impossible to find—"

"Melanie and Mark were lovers," Sydney interrupted, tired of the woman's sarcasm, "which resulted in her becoming pregnant."

That brought a frown. "What?"

Sydney gathered Reverend Hauff hadn't told her that part of it. "You didn't know?"

"I had no idea she was . . . the police didn't mention that to me. Wouldn't they—"

"She'd had an abortion."

"An abortion," Lillian Delacourt said wonderingly. "So, that was it." At Sydney's questioning look, she added, albeit grudgingly, "Some time ago, in late April I believe, Melanie came to me and said she had to have some money from her account."

"You handle the students' financial accounts?"

"Not usually. But since her father is so often out of the country and unreachable, he thought it prudent that Melanie have access to whatever money she might need, and he set up a trust account for her. She drew a weekly allowance, and also could get larger amounts if she wished."

"And in April she came to you to get money to pay for the abortion?"

"Yes. I didn't know it was for that reason, of course."

"What did she tell you the money was for?"

"She didn't." Her smile was disapproving. "Although I administered the trust, I was not permitted to ask what she intended to do with it. Even if I had known, it wouldn't have made any difference."

"Why not?"

"Because, like her father, Melanie Whitman was accountable to no one. The endowment her father bestowed upon the school guaranteed that. She did as she damned well pleased most of the time."

"But she was seventeen, legally a minor. Someone should have been watching out for her."

The headmistress picked up a pencil, made a notation on one of the papers on her desk, and put the pencil back down before responding.

"If you are suggesting I am somehow responsible for her affair with Mark Anderson, you are way out of line. Other than handcuffing myself to the girl, how could I hope to monitor her behavior?"

She had, Sydney realized, a valid point.

"And as for Mark Anderson, as long as he maintained a professional manner during the school day, I had no cause to inquire into his private life."

"The parents of the other girls might not see it that way. As a teacher, he is in a position of trust, and he violated that trust."

"Neither of us is naive enough to believe this is the first time a teacher has had an affair with a student. It happens. In this case—"

"In this case it ended in murder."

That silenced her.

"Reverend Hauff told me he came to you on Thursday afternoon after he'd talked to Melanie. Regarding a letter she had written?"

"Yes."

"There were, I understand, allegations regarding drugs and sexual coercion?"

"I didn't see the letter, but that is what he told me, yes."

"You told him you would handle it."

"Yes."

"And I know you called Mark Anderson into your office later that day."

After a moment's hesitation: "Yes."

Sydney saw the resignation in the headmistress's eyes. "What did you say to him, Miss Delacourt?"

"What would you have said? I told him he had to convince Melanie not to send the letter." She got up abruptly and went to the window. She stood, arms folded, staring out.

"Was he upset when you confronted him?"

"Of course, he was. He was shaking like a leaf. He denied he'd ever given Melanie drugs, or used them himself. He denied they had been physically intimate. He told me he was in love with her, and wanted to marry her."

"Did you believe him?"

"I wanted to." She turned from the window. "Maybe I did believe him. Melanie was a bright girl, but she wasn't by any means an easy person to deal with. She had a lot of emotional problems. It crossed my mind she was making it all up."

"You know, I've heard one person after another mention Melanie's problems. Everyone seemed to know about them, but no one did anything to help her. Except for Mark Anderson," she amended, "and even that turned out to be nothing more than a holding action."

"You may think me heartless, Miss Bryant, but I'm not. I've spent the past three days wondering if there was something else I could have done. It's easy for you to come in here after the fact and say, 'you should have done better,' but I did the best I could."

"It wasn't good enough."

"That isn't true. I—"

"Why didn't you call her into your office, Miss Delacourt? Why didn't you deal with the issue directly, instead of trying to 'handle it' by hushing it up? You owed it to Melanie Whitman and every other student at Hilyer Academy to conduct a full inquiry into the charges she was making."

"It's my job to protect the school."

"The hell with the school." Sydney got up to leave, but she stopped at the door. "You've been doing your best to keep the lid on this, to keep it quiet, but I don't believe it's really the school you want to protect. I think you're covering your own ass, because it never would have come to this if you'd done what you should have done in the first place."

"That isn't—"

"Melanie was crying out for help. And no one heard her. Because no one was listening."

CHAPTER THIRTY-EIGHT

"Sydney?"

"Hmm?"

"Are you all right? You've been staring off into space for ages."

Sydney looked at Nicole, who was sitting cross-legged on the floor, surrounded by books. "I'm fine," she said. "I'm just thinking about tomorrow."

Nicole frowned. "Me too. I haven't been to a funeral since my mother's. I don't remember much about it . . . I was only six."

"Would you rather not go?"

"I've got to go," Nicole said. She closed the book she was holding and put it aside. "I have to."

"All right. If you're sure."

"I am. You'll be there, won't you?"

Sydney nodded. "And Ethan will pick you up at the school at one."

"Good. Then if I do something like *faint* again, he can catch me."

Although she'd said it lightly, Sydney could tell it worried Nicole. "Or if he faints, you can catch him."

"Sydney," Nicole said, and giggled.

Nicole went to bed at ten and Sydney found herself at loose ends again.

She hated feeling this way.

She had notes she could type up from her interviews with Rachel Dillon and Reverend Hauff, but she doubted she could concentrate long enough to finish. She'd tried to read the Sunday paper earlier, and found herself re-reading the same paragraph over and over. Even after she'd read it half a dozen times, she wasn't sure what it had said.

She wandered into the kitchen and stood in front of the refrigerator, although she wasn't hungry. When the motor came on, she shut the door.

Back in the living room she turned on the television, and tried to get interested in the Sunday night movie. It was a murder mystery, her favorite type of film, but it was halfway through and she hadn't a clue what was going on. After a few minutes, she gave up.

"Damn it," she said and shut off the set. She immediately turned it back on, crossed to the couch and sat down.

She watched intently for about thirty seconds before realizing it was a commercial and not the movie at all. She had been trying to figure out the plot of a telephone commercial.

She gave up.

If staring into space was the only way to deal with her restlessness, she would stare into space.

There was, she admitted to herself, something in the death of Melanie Whitman that didn't fit. Maybe more than one something.

The problem she had with Mark Anderson as the killer was her absolute certainty he had truly loved Melanie. Granted, he hadn't been forthcoming about his involvement with her, but that may have been an attempt on his part to protect the girl's reputation.

He would keep her on the pedestal as long as he had a breath in him.

And no matter what the provocation, Sydney could not see him doing what had been done to Melanie. Perhaps in a rage he could have struck her once, but twice? And so hard he had, as Mitch said, 'loosened her teeth'? That gentle man?

It didn't feel right to her.

"Wait a minute," she said, unaware she'd spoken aloud.

Mark Anderson was definitely the one, wasn't he? Wasn't he?

Rachel Dillon had seen him kissing Melanie.

Reverend Hauff had said their relationship was no secret.

Jeff King contended Mark was 'a little nuts' about her.

Even Nicole, who thought King was the killer,

had said Melanie was Anderson's favorite student.

On the other hand, Lillian Delacourt thought it was more likely Melanie had fallen for Jeff King. But no, that wasn't true. The headmistress had called Mark Anderson in to confront him with Melanie's allegations, not King.

For whatever reasons, Sandra Lockwood hadn't thought either man was the one; but even she had finally agreed that it was at least possible Mark was interested.

He had to be the one.

Didn't he?

"But," she said, getting up to pace, "what about Jeff King?"

King and his remark about some other man giving Melanie what Mark Anderson couldn't?

King, whose "nature" it was to flirt?

With his movie star looks and a magnetism about him even she had felt? His casual sexuality, and his thinly disguised conceit?

What about Jeff King?

CHAPTER THIRTY-NINE

Monday, June 12th

The private security guards Lillian Delacourt had hired were nowhere in sight when Sydney and Nicole arrived at Hilyer Academy, but what was obviously an unmarked police car was parked—crookedly—in the lot.

"I'll come in with you," Sydney said. With only the one car, it wasn't likely anything major was happening, but just in case . . .

Nicole looked at her curiously, but didn't comment. She grabbed her backpack, draped the navy blue dress she'd chosen to wear to the funeral over her arm, took a deep breath and started resolutely toward the building.

Sydney walked beside her. The girl had been quiet this morning, no doubt due in part to the upcoming funeral; but there was, she thought, more to it than that. "What is it, Nicole?"

Nicole glanced at her sideways. "What?"

"You haven't said two words all morning."

"Oh, I'm just worried about my finals."

She didn't quite buy that, but she smiled sympathetically. "You'll do fine."

"Hmm. I'd better. I was at the store the other day, you know?"

"Yes?"

"There was this lady putting new advertisements in the little mini-billboard things they put on front of shopping carts. You know what I mean?"

"I've seen them."

"Well, if I don't get into the right college, that'll be the kind of job I'm qualified for," Nicole said glumly. "Going from store to store stuffing cereal ads in shopping carts."

Sydney laughed. "Listen, if it gets that bad, you can come and work for me."

"Really?"

"Absolutely. You'd make a great P.I."

They were nearing the front door, and Nicole stopped suddenly. "Sydney, I can't believe it was Mr. Anderson. I just can't."

"I know, honey." She'd spent hours trying to make sense of all of it, with limited success. She put her arm around the girl's shoulder and gave it a squeeze. "Try not to think about Mr. Anderson."

"I have my English final this morning. How am I *not* going to think about him?"

It was a good question, and she had no answer for it.

"What if the police come in and arrest him right in the middle of class?"

"They wouldn't do that."

"I hope not." Nicole frowned. "God, I hope not."

They were all in the hall outside Lillian Delacourt's office when Sydney and Nicole went inside.

Sandra Lockwood, Theadora Fairweather, Jeff King, Rachel Dillon, and a bespectacled woman with a faintly imperious manner turned in their direction.

The headmistress apparently had been speaking, but she stopped when she saw them.

Beside her, Nicole stiffened.

"Nicole," Lillian Delacourt said, "go on to your classroom, please."

Nicole seemed incapable of movement, and Sydney gave her a gentle push. "Go on."

The girl might have just been learning to walk. She moved as if afraid her legs wouldn't hold her.

No one said anything. Nicole disappeared around a corner, and a moment later they heard the sound of a door opening and closing.

"Miss Bryant," Lillian Delacourt said, taking a step forward. "There is a police officer in my office with a warrant giving him permission to review the personnel records of all of the staff."

"Yes?"

"Would you happen to know why, if . . . if they have a suspect . . . which you seem to feel they might . . . why they want to see *all* of our records?"

"This is an outrage," the woman wearing

glasses said. "I was in the library the entire time. Nicole was there with me. Why look at my file?"

"I don't know." Sydney glanced at Mark Anderson; he looked as though he hadn't slept. His expression conveyed his exhaustion and, underlying that, resignation?

Even so, he gave her a faint smile.

King, on the other hand, showed his displeasure in the clench of his jaw. "I think you should call the school's attorney, Lillian."

"An attorney won't be much help," Sydney said, but in fact she wondered at the tactics of the police. A search warrant was required by law to specify the things or persons which it directed the police to seize. And probable cause had to be established.

At that point the door behind them opened, and a detective Sydney recognized as belonging to the homicide team came out.

He was one of the bulldog variety of cop: solidly built, but with a double chin that might have given a miscreant the false and very foolish impression he was soft. He walked lightly for a big man, and he bounced on the balls of his feet as he regarded them.

"Thanks. I got what I was looking for." He patted his suit pocket.

"Officer," Lillian began. "I want to know—"

The cop's smile was sardonic. It stopped her cold. "We'll be in touch," he said. He nodded at Sydney as he passed.

"Well, I never!" the librarian said after the detective was gone.

"I believe that." Sandra Lockwood's eyes were

still fixed on the door, as if she looked hard enough, she could burn right through it with her fiery stare, and maybe through the cop as well.

"You can stand around if you want," Jeff King said, "but I'm calling a lawyer."

"No, you're not." The headmistress did nothing to conceal her displeasure. "Your students are waiting. All of you . . . go to class."

Sydney caught a look pass between Sandra Lockwood and Jeff King, and saw Sandra mouth the word, "bitch." But no one argued.

CHAPTER FORTY

Sydney walked along the pathway toward the library.

Perhaps she was overly sensitive to it, but she thought there was something, a feeling, about the place echoing still with the violence that had occurred.

More than eighty hours after Melanie Whitman had taken her last breath, the trees rustled and sighed.

The police were long since finished here. The groundsmen had scrubbed the stone walk and raked away the leaves. If the grass had been trampled, there was no sign of it now.

No one would know a girl had died here.

Sydney paused, listening. It was cool in the shade, and fragrant with acacia blossoms. Even in the early morning, the branches of the trees filtered the light.

After a minute, she went on.

*   *   *

Melanie Whitman's Chevrolet IROC was indeed parked in a small lot behind the library.

The driver's door was locked. She circled to the passenger door not expecting to find it open, and it wasn't. The window was rolled down a couple of inches, but not far enough to allow her arm through.

She would need a slim-jim to get into the car. Or, she thought, an extra key.

Without giving a thought to her clean linen slacks, she kneeled in the dirt and gravel beside the right front fenderwell, and reached up beneath it. There was hard-caked dried mud all along the metal, but nothing else.

She ducked her head to peek under the front quarter panel, but there was no little magnetic key case.

Sydney got up and went to the front of the car, looking critically at it. She wondered what percentage of the bumper was made of fiberglass or plastic? The magnet wouldn't stick to either.

She ran her hand along the underside of the bumper anyway, but came up empty.

A search of the left front fenderwell—usually a good bet as a location for extra keys—also revealed nothing, except a spot or two of rust.

Sydney lay on the ground and scooted until her head and one shoulder were under the frame. She studied the undercarriage of the car, looking for the familiar shape of a key box.

And hit pay dirt.

It wasn't clinging to anything, though. Melanie Whitman hadn't apparently trusted its magnetic properties. She had used silver duct tape to hold it onto a coil spring.

As she worked to get it free, she heard the gravel being crunched as someone walked toward her. She resisted the urge to look and see who it was, instead concentrating on tearing through the duct tape.

"Sydney?"

Mitch. "Hold on," she said. The damn thing was almost free.

"Are you looking for these?"

Sydney turned her head. All she could see of him were his pants legs, shoes, and one hand. Between his thumb and forefinger dangled a set of keys.

"Shit," she said. Irritation helped her yank the key box free. She wiggled out from under the rocker panel, the gravel digging into her back.

Mitch offered her a hand up. "I like a woman who's not afraid to get dirty," he said.

"Where were you five minutes ago?" She handed him the key box before he could ask for it, and began to brush at the dirt on her slacks.

"I was waiting for the tow truck."

She saw his car parked across the road in the shade of a big oak. "You were there all along? Watching me crawl around on my hands and knees?"

Mitch smiled, but said nothing.

"You couldn't come over and say, 'Oh, Sydney, that isn't necessary. I have the keys'?"

"Oh, Sydney," he said.

"Shut up."

Mitch laughed. "You worked so hard for it, I'll

275

let you open the door." He dropped the key ring into her hand. "And you don't even have to thank me."

"I won't."

The car was clean inside, as though it had just been vacuumed. It would be gone over thoroughly at impound later; but for now, they looked in the glove compartment, in the center console, and under the two front seats.

The current registration and proof of insurance were in a plastic bag in the glove compartment; along with a map of California, the lock adapter for the car's customized wheels, and a flashlight with a cracked lens and no batteries.

The console held only a small pot of lip gloss and a mascara wand, which Mitch looked at with a frown.

"Don't tell me," he said, "she was one of those ladies who put her makeup on in the rear view mirror while she was driving?"

Sydney pushed the front passenger seat forward, and got into the rather claustropohic back area. Again on her hands and knees, she peered under the driver's seat.

There was nothing in sight, but she knew from her own car that things sometimes got caught in the thicker pile carpet beneath the seat.

"Wait a minute, Mitch," she said. "Do you have an envelope?"

"What is it?"

"I don't know." She could only see something

white on the dark red carpet.

He gave her a glassine envelope. "Do it right, kid."

She positioned the opening of the envelope at the edge of the object, then reached beyond it to pull up the carpet just enough so whatever it was rolled inside. When she brought it out she saw it was a small glass vial with a white rubber stopper.

"Well, what do you know?" Mitch took the envelope and held it up to the light. "Maybe a little residue in there, what do you think?"

"Cocaine?"

"That'd be my guess. There's trouble in River City for sure."

Sydney thought back to what Reverend Hauff had said about Melanie's letter. "Damn it."

"What's wrong?"

"I just don't see Mark Anderson introducing Melanie to cocaine."

Mitch shrugged. "You'd be surprised at the people who are snorting this stuff." He sealed the envelope, initialed it, and slipped it into his shirt pocket. "Let's take a look at the trunk."

He pulled and held the front seat forward so she could get out of the car. For a moment they stood within inches of each other, before she moved away.

Mitch smiled and followed her to the back of the car. "You missed a spot," he said.

"What?" She selected a key to try in the trunk and inserted it in the lock.

"You have dirt on your slacks. I'll be glad to brush it off—"

The trunk sprung open, and they saw it at the same time: a tiny, black velvet ring box laying open and on its side.

"I thought women were sentimental about these things," he said.

Sydney didn't comment. She watched as Mitch picked it up and pulled out the cardboard inset.

Folded and tucked inside was a receipt.

He pulled a plastic bag similar to a sandwich bag out of his jacket pocket, put everything inside, and sealed it. "Well, we'll let the evidence techs see whose name is on this receipt. But I guess we both know who it is."

CHAPTER FORTY-ONE

At one o'clock, Sydney finished typing the last
f the interviews on the Whitman case. From what
Mitch had told her when they parted at the school,
: looked very likely an arrest warrant would be
ssued sometime today charging Mark Anderson
with murder.

All morning long she'd been on edge, expecting
he phone to ring with the news they had picked
im up, but it hadn't.

What, she wondered, was going on?

Even if there hadn't been a name on the receipt
n the ring box, the odds were good the police
evidence technicians had been able to lift usable
rints from it. And if there *had* been a name . . .

It would establish once and for all who
Melanie's lover had been.

Not that there was much doubt.

Sydney sighed. She put the interviews in the
older, and filed it away. There was nothing more
or her to do. With an arrest imminent, the case

was, officially, out of her hands.

After a stop at her apartment to change clothes, she drove to the church where Melanie Whitman's funeral services would be held.

There were a number of reporters gathered on the street, including a camera crew from the CBS affiliate, and of course, Victor Griffith. That didn't surprise her. The funeral of the murdered daughter of a rich man couldn't help but be a good draw.

Dozens of black limousines filled the available parking, and she had to circle the block to find a spot in which to squeeze the Mustang.

Victor lumbered toward her as she approached the church. "Nice day for a funeral," he said, falling into step beside her.

She glanced at him. "Is there such a thing?"

"I did send roses, by the way."

In all the years she'd been acquainted with him, she'd never known him to do anything even remotely decent. Sydney was touched. "That was nice of you."

"I know." He grinned sheepishly. "But don't tell anyone . . . I have a reputation to consider."

"Don't worry, Victor, your secret is safe. No one would believe me anyway."

"Good." He stopped as they reached the stairs. "Listen, Sydney, I've got to wait out here for the grieving father—"

"He's not here yet?"

"I'm sure he wants to be fashionably late."

280

"To his daughter's funeral?"

"Hey, take a look around," he said, "we're talking, 'film at eleven' here. Tonight there'll be footage of the bereaved father, and he may even make the front—"

"I've got to go."

"Hey, what's wrong?"

"Think about it," she said, and ran up the stairs.

She found Nicole and Ethan in one of the back rows. The church was packed, but they'd managed to save room for her. She sat between them.

Nicole looked pale but determined, and she attempted a smile.

"Are you okay?" Sydney whispered.

"I don't know. Ask me later. Maybe in September."

A murmur rippled through the crowd, and Sydney turned to see Albert Whitman come through the door. A second later, the organist began to play.

He looked mildly bored as he surveyed the church, and then walked slowly up the aisle. If he felt anything at all, it didn't show on his face.

The service began.

The smell of flowers was almost overwhelming. Midway through the service, Sydney realized Nicole had begun breathing rapidly, in shallow little gasps.

"Take it easy," she said, as quietly as she could.

"You're hyperventilating."

"I have . . . to get out."

Sydney and Ethan exchanged a glance.

Ethan stood up and helped Nicole to her feet. "Can you walk?"

Tears glistened in her eyes. "I'll try." But she took one step, and the color drained from her face.

Ethan lifted her into his arms. "Come on, let's get her out of here."

Sydney followed them.

The fresh air revived Nicole within a few minutes. Thankfully, the reporters showed no interest in them, and they sat on the steps in the shade.

Nicole had given up trying to hold back her tears. She covered her eyes with her hands and cried until nothing more would come.

CHAPTER FORTY-TWO

"Do you remember me?" a voice said.

Sydney turned to see Orenthal O'Shea looking somber in a dark suit. "Of course, Mr. O'Shea. How are you?"

"Ah. There's something wrong with an old man like me being at a young girl's funeral." He sighed. "Your friends left?"

"Yes." At her insistence, Ethan had taken Nicole home. Nicole had protested, but Sydney had seen the relief in her eyes. It had been the right thing to do.

"She was Melly's friend?"

Sydney nodded.

"He's a piece of work, isn't he?"

She didn't have to look to know he was referring to Albert Whitman, who had been surrounded by the press, and was holding up the funeral procession to the gravesite while he talked with them. A young blond in a black dress and veil stood beside him.

"If God wills it, I'm going to live to dance on *his* grave," O'Shea said. "Or piss on it."

"I wouldn't waste good piss."

O'Shea ducked his head and smiled. "You're right. Do you know what they were doing last night in a house of mourning?"

"What?"

O'Shea nodded his head toward Whitman. "The ice maiden has a Russian wolfhound. She was trying to teach it how to catch a frisbee. They were laughing their damned fool heads off."

Albert Whitman stood through the brief graveside service, his hands clasped behind his back. The blond sat in one of the chairs usually reserved for family.

Off to one side, standing alone, Sydney watched them both and wondered if the man felt anything. From the expression on his face, he might have been a visitor from a foreign country, observing the quaint local customs with a hint of amusement.

What would it take, she wondered, to shock that look from those eyes?

She waited until he was by himself and walked up to him. "Mr. Whitman?"

Perhaps he thought she was a reporter, because he turned to her with a smile. "Yes?"

"Do you know that her skull was fractured?"

"What?"

"I asked you if you know that Melanie's skull was fractured."

There was no immediate reaction. After a moment, he nodded. "Yes," he said, "I know."

"And that your daughter died alone—"

"We all die alone."

"—after living alone for most of her life?"

He looked at her more closely. "What is it you want?"

"I want you to mourn your daughter."

"I see." Whitman ran a hand down the lapel of his expensive tailored suit, then adjusted the cuffs. "May I ask what concern it is of yours?"

"I'm a private investigator, and I've spent four days trying to find out who killed Melanie."

"Oh?"

"In doing so, I've learned a lot about her, things I am sure you don't know—"

"I dare say you're right."

"—and apparently don't care to know."

He laughed softly. "I suppose you feel it's your duty to tell me these things. Even though there's really no point to it, is there? I mean, she is *dead*."

Sydney could not remember ever despising anyone as much as she did this man, but she kept her temper. "No, Mr. Whitman, I'm not."

"Oh." He glanced at his watch. "Then I suppose you're going to tell me to go to hell."

"If I thought hell would have you, I might. But then, there goes the neighborhood."

"It's been very . . . entertaining, but now I must ask you to excuse me."

He started off and she reached out to grab his

arm. "Someone else murdered Melanie, but you're the one who killed her. If she hadn't been so desperate for someone to love her, she might be alive right now."

"Thank you for your insight," he said, freeing himself from her grasp, and was gone.

"It didn't do any good, did it?"

"No, Mr. O'Shea, it didn't."

They watched as Albert Whitman disappeared into his limousine. The chauffeur closed the door and sprinted around to the other side.

"But you tried," O'Shea said.

Sydney frowned. "That and a dime . . ."

The limousine pulled away. Its smoked windows hid Whitman from view; but she would bet he'd already forgotten what she'd said; that his mind was on dinner; or the next blond; or anything except his daughter's body being lowered into her grave.

"I used to think it would be good for Melly if he was home more," O'Shea said, "but now I wonder if she wasn't better off without him. Maybe being a latchkey child wasn't the worst thing after all."

Sydney looked at him. "A latchkey child?"

"Sure. Melly wore her housekeys on a chain around her neck . . ."

"Keys," she whispered, and all at once a lot of things began to make sense.

CHAPTER FORTY-THREE

Sydney made it to Mira Mesa in record time.

There were no patrol cars around, which meant either they'd already picked him up and were gone, or the wheels of justice were grinding slowly, and they hadn't been here yet.

She was counting on it being the latter of the two possibilities.

She rang the doorbell, pushing the button hard and releasing it three times in rapid succession in an attempt to signal her urgency.

"Come on, Mark" she said impatiently, and raised her hand to pound on the door. Then she heard the dead bolt being thrown.

The door opened and Mark Anderson looked out at her. "Well," he said without emotion, "I was expecting it to be the police."

"I'd like to talk to you."

He smiled faintly and used his forefinger to push his glasses up on the bridge of his nose. "I don't know if I should be saying anything at this point."

"May I come in?"

"If you wish." He stood aside.

The front room was exactly as she had last seen it. The glass of iced coffee he'd given her was still sitting where she'd put it down. A thin film floated on top of the murky liquid.

He followed her glance. "Hmm. I guess the maid must have more days off than I thought."

"Mark, you know that the police suspect you of killing Melanie."

"Yes."

"But you didn't do it, did you?"

He didn't answer. Instead he sat heavily in the chair and leaned forward, resting his elbows on his knees and staring at the floor.

"You loved her," Sydney said.

"Yes."

"You wanted to marry her."

"Of course."

"And you'd given her an engagement ring."

He sighed. "I bought the ring from a friend of mine. He manages a small jewelry store. He gave me a good price, and he let me take it before I'd finished paying for it. I still owe him money." He looked at her. "I have a check due me from the school. Do you think the police will let me pay the ring off?"

"Mark—"

"I know they know about the ring. My friend called and told me a couple of detectives were in this afternoon asking about it. They had the sales slip—I gave the receipt to Melanie so she could have the ring sized if it didn't fit—and, of course, he had to tell them what they wanted to know. They'll be here soon, don't you think?"

"Yes, I imagine they will."

"I thought after I hung up from talking to him that maybe I should make a run for it, go to Mexico or something. Maybe I could teach English in South America. But . . . I'm not the desperado type. So, here I am."

"About the ring you bought her . . . she didn't have it on her when her body was found. Do you know what might have happened to it?"

He frowned and shook his head.

"I know," Sydney went on, "from what one of her friends told me she wore it on a chain around her neck."

"Yes. When I proposed to her, I slipped it on her finger, but she didn't want anyone to know about us. She didn't want to get me in trouble with the school. So she wore it around her neck instead."

"With her house keys?"

Mark looked at her curiously. "Yes. How did you know that?"

She didn't answer, saying instead. "Mark, I want you to tell me about Melanie."

His confusion showed. "But I have."

"No. Her teacher, Mr. Anderson, told me about his bright and talented student. I want to hear about Melanie from Mark, the man who was in love with her. There is a difference."

"I did love her," he said quietly. "From the very first time I saw her. She wasn't as beautiful then, but she had a quality about her that was special."

289

Sydney could see in his eyes this wasn't easy for him.

But he smiled to himself, as if remembering. "I suppose it might have been that I recognized her as another of the walking wounded. A kindred spirit. A lost child. But whatever it was, we *knew* each other from the moment our eyes met."

"She knew how you felt about her, even then?"

"Oh yes. I wanted to make the hurt go away. I wasn't sure how to go about it—I haven't much experience at being happy—but that was my intention."

"Did you succeed, do you think?"

Mark considered for a moment before answering. "I think she wasn't *as* sad. And she *was* happy when I gave her the ring."

"At Christmas?"

"A couple of weeks before, actually."

"What happened then?"

"What makes you think anything did?"

Sydney held his eyes. "Something must have. Something changed. Tell me."

"Well. I guess it started when Melanie had some trouble in chemistry."

"King's class."

"Yes. It was odd, because she'd never had any problems before. But all of a sudden, she was having to spend a lot of time at it."

She nodded encouragement for him to go on.

"Apparently, King had told her in no uncertain terms she was in danger of failing if she didn't put more time in."

"When was this?" she asked, thinking of what

King had said about Melanie spacing-out during the mid-term.

"Early in the quarter. The second or third week."

"Before mid-term?"

"Yes. Anyway, he pretty much said that if she wanted to pass the class, she would have to devote most of her free time to studying. Put extra hours in at the lab. And he offered to tutor her."

From the way he said it, tutor was a dirty word. "What did you think about that?"

"I didn't like it," he said. "I missed seeing her, and I may as well admit I was jealous she was spending so much time with him."

"How much time?"

"I didn't keep track, but . . . a lot."

"Had she been staying with you on weekends?"

"I saw her occasionally on weekends, but she didn't stay with me."

"Where was she? If she wasn't at home, or on campus, or with you, where was she?"

"I thought this past year she and another of the girls were sharing a small apartment. I was mistaken. I don't know where she was, or who she was with."

"It might have been Jeff King?"

"It might have been," he agreed.

"When we first talked, you told me Melanie saw through him . . . that she wasn't taken in by him at all."

"That's what she told me."

"So why were you jealous of him?"

"Because I know he's not the type of a man who

gives up. He takes what he wants, regardless of the consequences. I knew he'd keep after her, and keep after her, and would say or do anything to get what he wanted. I was afraid she might not always be able to say no."

Sydney hesitated. "Do you think, being together so much, at some point they became intimate?"

A pained look crossed his face. "I think so. It had to have been him."

She remembered the look on his face on Saturday when she had revealed that the police believed Melanie had had a lover. She didn't want to mention the pregnancy if she could help it. He was hurting bad enough already.

"You loved Melanie," she said after a moment had passed, "but you weren't lovers."

"No, we weren't. We were going to be married, and I had waited for her for so long . . . but no. I never made love to Melanie." He looked down at his clasped hands. "I wish now I had."

"Mark . . . what you said earlier. About not being the desperado type. Why haven't you run? If you know the police are after you?"

"Well, it doesn't matter, does it? If they arrest me, I'll either go to jail or I won't. Without Melanie, my life isn't really worth much." He gestured around him. "This is it. This is what I have, and it doesn't amount to anything without her."

"But you didn't kill her."

"No, I didn't."

"Don't you want to know who did?"

His smile was cynical. "I know who killed her,

and I think you do too. Still, I can protect Melanie by not protesting my innocence."

"But Mark—"

"Let them think I killed her during a lover's quarrel. At least I truly loved her. She wasn't someone I used, and grew tired of, and couldn't get rid of. I can't stand to have anyone think of her that way. And that's what it would come to."

"You can't let her killer go free."

He didn't seem to have heard her. "Wherever she was those days and nights, they'd call it a love nest and her a blond coed. It'll be like that sordid mess in New York . . . those two rich kids in the park."

"You're willing to risk a murder one rap to protect Melanie's reputation?"

"Oh, yes."

"But why? If she betrayed you with another man?"

"Because I loved her unconditionally, and there is nothing she could ever say or do to change that. I am sorry she didn't come to me and tell me about Jeff face-to-face, but I understand why she didn't. She didn't know about forgiveness. She never forgave her father or mother, so I guess she couldn't comprehend such a thing."

"No. . . ."

His smile was wistful. "I would have forgiven her. I would have still married her."

Sydney believed him.

CHAPTER FORTY-FOUR

Sydney left Mark Anderson as she had found him; waiting stoically for the police.

Traffic on Miramar Road was essentially at a standstill, but when she tried to bypass it by taking Mira Mesa Boulevard she found more of the same. With no viable alternative, she had no choice but to inch along at five miles an hour with the rest of them.

The only good thing about the traffic was it gave her time to think.

And remember.

First, things that Mitch had told her:

"There was one thing that was a little odd. The girl was clutching a broken necklace in her right hand. A gold chain."

"There were marks on her neck where it had been ripped off her."

"It was practically embedded in her flesh."

And what Amber had not quite said:

'*I saw she was wearing a ring on that necklace she*

always wore, with the—"

Keys?

In her mind's eye, she saw Nicole pulling the chain around her neck to reveal the keys to her and the Halpern's apartments.

And this afternoon at the funeral, Orenthal O'Shea:

"Melly wore her housekeys on a chain around her neck . . ."

It hadn't been the ring Melanie's killer was after, but the keys around her neck.

The keys to her house.

Her house which had been burglarized the night she was killed.

What were the odds that it had been a coincidence?

"Sometime last night someone tossed Melanie's room. And only her room. Searching for something probably. What they were looking for, I don't know, nor do I know whether they found it."

He'd ripped the keys from her neck so that he could get into her house. He had gone through her room, looking for what?

Reverend Hauff had said Melanie had indicated that she had been given drugs by one of her teachers. The vial in the girl's car seemed to offer confirmation.

"We've had more than a few girls come back, sick from drinking and heaven knows what else," Theadora Fairweather had said.

It wasn't a relationship the killer was trying to hide.

It had something to do with drugs.

296

CHAPTER FORTY-FIVE

Sydney pulled the Mustang into her parking space, and reached to turn off the ignition when someone tapped on her window. She nearly jumped out of her skin.

Victor Griffith grinned at her and waved.

"You scared the life out of me," she said, getting out of the car.

"Hey, I thought you might have a comment since Travis is crediting you with making a break in the case."

"What are you talking about?" She started up the walk toward the building.

"Come off it, Sydney. They're going to arrest the guy right now."

"Damn." She should have stopped at a gas station and phoned Mitch to tell him what she'd found out. Well, she'd call him as soon as she got inside.

"What was that?"

"Nothing."

He loped along beside her. "I heard you, you said 'damn.'"

At the gate she turned to him. "Victor, I have no statement, nothing to say." She pulled the gate across, locking him out. "See you later."

"Hey," he called after her, "did you know this guy had gotten kicked out of his last job for the very same thing?"

That stopped her cold, and she faced him. "What are you talking about?"

"Not murder, but the other. You know, engaging in sex with an underage female."

She stared at him. "You're not talking about Mark Anderson . . ."

"Anderson? Hell no. The other one, King."

"They're arresting Jeff King?"

"Wait a minute," Victor said, motioning 'stop' by holding up his hands. "If you broke this case, how come you're asking me whether they're arresting King? Didn't you know?"

She walked back to the gate. "No, I didn't."

"Huh. Well, there's a first."

"Where did you hear this news?"

"I got lucky. I just happen to know this secretary —don't worry, Sydney, she doesn't mean a thing to me—who typed up the arrest warrant."

"When was this?"

"What do you mean, 'when was this?' Maybe half an hour ago." He looked at the watch on his bony wrist. "They ought to be picking lover boy up right this minute."

She thought about it for a moment and nodded with satisfaction. "Thanks, Victor."

"Hey! A comment?"

"I'd like to help you out, but since I haven't the faintest idea what Lieutenant Travis is talking about when he says I broke the case, there's nothing I can tell you. I'll have to owe you one."

Victor wrapped his fingers around the wrought iron bars and rattled the gate. "I'm gonna hold you to it, Sydney."

"I know you will."

The cat was sitting in front of her door and she reached down to scratch his ears.

"How you been, Trouble?"

He meowed.

"Me too." She tried the door, but it was locked. "Did Nicole go out?" she asked the cat.

He blinked.

She dug the keys out of her purse. When she opened the door, Trouble ran in around her legs. He made a beeline for the kitchen and squeezed through the swinging door.

"Nicole?"

The apartment was silent. The shades had been pulled down; it was dark and cool inside. She crossed to the end table and turned on a lamp.

"Nicole?"

Maybe she was sleeping. Sydney walked to the bedroom door which was slightly ajar. She pushed it further open; the creak sounded abnormally loud.

It was even darker than the front room, but she could see that there was no one on the bed.

Sydney looked at the bathroom. The door was closed and there was no light showing underneath.

Unless Nicole was in the kitchen, she wasn't in the apartment.

Trouble was perched on the counter next to the cookie jar. His green eyes caught the light when she pushed open the door.

"She's not here, is she?" Sydney got a chocolate-chip cookie from the jar and broke it into pieces. She offered him a piece which he took delicately from her hand. The rest she put on the counter.

Nicole had probably gone down to her own apartment and own bed. It was understandable she would seek whatever comfort she could find after being as upset as she'd been this afternoon.

She took the last cookie with her into the front room.

"Lieutenant Travis, please," she said when she got through to the division.

"He's out in the field."

"What about the detective heading the Melanie Whitman case?"

"Sorry. Sergeant Young is in the field."

"Is there anyone I can talk to?"

"Well, the cleaning lady's here . . . everyone else is in the field."

"It must be crowded," she said.

"Pardon?"

"The field."

"You want to leave a message?"

"Thanks, I'll call back."

Sydney went down the hall to the Halpern apartment and knocked on the door.

"Nicole?" She knocked harder, then pushed the bell. "It's Sydney."

There was no response.

The door was locked.

"I'll feel safer locked inside," Nicole had said yesterday.

Was she in there?

There was no light showing in the apartment that she could see.

Still . . . Nicole hadn't been sleeping well for the past few nights. As tired as she must be, she might not wake easily.

Or she could have escaped into deep thought, as she had the other night. If she could tune out three of her friends talking, she could tune out a knock on the door. Or a doorbell.

Or anything short of cannon fire.

Sydney let go of the doorknob, walked back to her own apartment and went straight to the telephone. Maybe a ringing phone would wake her. She was, after all, a teenage girl.

But the line rang unanswered. Sydney counted fifteen rings, hung up and dialed again—this time Ethan's number.

"Ethan," she said when he answered. "Is Nicole with you?"

"No, why would she be with me?"

"She isn't here. I thought she might be in her apartment, but she's not. Did she say anything about going out when you brought her home from the funeral this afternoon?"

"Not a word. She said she was going to lay down for awhile, maybe take a nap, and then study for her finals tomorrow."

Sydney frowned, her eyes searching the front room. Nicole's backpack was gone. Had it been in the bedroom? She didn't recall seeing it there.

"Maybe one of her friends called," Ethan was saying. "And they're studying together."

"But she'd leave a note . . ."

"And she didn't?"

"Not that I can see." She looked for the pad she usually kept by the phone, but didn't find it. "Maybe she went out to study by the pool. Or she went to another movie to try and cheer herself up. Or she got hungry and hijacked a grocery truck."

Ethan laughed. "Do you want me to come over and help you look for her?"

"No, that's all right, but thanks anyway."

"Anytime. And if you need me, just call."

She hung up, but kept her hand on the phone. debating whether to call Hilyer Academy. Maybe one of her friends knew where she was.

The number, when she tried, was busy.

Sydney heard a sound behind her and turned her head slightly, listening.

Trouble jumped up on the back of the couch,

and began to lick at his paw.

She let out her breath in a sigh.

Sydney found the note in the refrigerator when she went to get a Pepsi.

> Went to the library
> Back by 5
>
>   Nicole

It was nearly seven o'clock.

CHAPTER FORTY-SIX

The lot behind the school library was empty when Sydney arrived to look for Nicole. Where, she wondered, was the librarian's car?

She started toward the building, the gravel crunching under her boots as she walked.

A car turned onto the narrow street, and she was briefly caught in the sweep of its headlights. The car drove slowly past.

Sydney turned up the collar of her denim jacket against the cool wind, and put her hands in her pockets. Her fingers closed around something metal and she pulled it out. It was her gold pen. She'd wondered where it had gone to.

When she reached the side of the building, she looked up to see if the lights were on, and was reassured when they were.

Nicole had probably lost track of the time.

She rounded the corner to the front of the building and ran up the steps. The library doors were inset with glass, but were covered by shades.

The door handle was an old-fashioned type she remembered from her own days at school with a flat lever at the top which usually took both hands to push down. For a moment she thought it was locked, but it clicked loudly and the door opened.

The air was musty and smelled of paper, pencil shavings, and that institutional paste only schools seem to use. She wrinkled her nose.

There was, she saw, no one at the front desk.

An open ink pad and date stamp were the only items on the green desk blotter.

"Hello?" she said.

No one answered.

"Nicole?" She took a step further into the room. "Is anyone here?"

She heard footsteps from somewhere, and tilted her head to listen.

"Sydney?"

Nicole appeared at the end of one of the aisles, an open book in her hands. She looked a little dazed, and as she stood there, she seemed to sway slightly.

"Are you all right?" Sydney asked. She slipped her bag off her shoulder and set it on the desk.

"Me? I'm fine."

"Do you know what time it is?"

Nicole frowned and shook her head.

"Where is the librarian?"

"Miss Shanfield?" Nicole glanced at the desk as though expecting to see the woman there. "I don't know. She was here a little while ago."

"I think," Sydney said, crossing the room, "that it's time we went home."

"But I've got more stuff to look up. Mr. King's tests are killers—"

"I wouldn't worry about it." She took the book from Nicole's hands and closed it. "Mr. King isn't going to be giving any more tests."

Given how exhausted and distracted Nicole looked, Sydney hadn't expected her to react, but the girl's eyes widened.

"What happened?"

"He's been arrested." She glanced at the number on the spine of the book and started down the aisle looking for a place to reshelve it.

"I knew it, I just knew it" Nicole said. "I told you it was him. But how did they find out? Weren't they after Mr. Anderson?"

"I wish I could tell you." Sydney found a corresponding empty space on the shelf and slipped the book in. "But I don't know myself."

Nicole had followed her into the aisle, and she stood with one hand resting on either shelf. "You will tell me, though, when you find out?"

"Sure."

They heard the sound of the library door opening. Nicole raised her eyebrows and made a face, then took two steps backward so she was at the end of the aisle. "Miss Shanfield," she said, "I'm—"

"Nicole," a man's voice said. "I've been looking for you."

It was Jeff King.

Nicole made a tiny motion with her hand, waving Sydney back, and stepped out of the aisle. "Really? I've been here all afternoon."

Sydney moved as quietly as possible up the aisle, and sat on her heels a foot short of the end. Luckily, the books on the lower shelves were tall enough that they blocked her from view. But neither could she see him.

"I think you have something I want."

"I do?"

"Yes. Terri said you have Melanie's lab note-book. That she gave it to you Thursday night?"

"Oh. Yes, I guess she did."

Nicole was doing her best to sound normal, but Sydney could hear the strain in her voice.

"I'd like to have it, if you don't mind."

King took a step forward and Sydney pressed herself against the shelf.

"Okay, sure. It's in my backpack."

Sydney saw the backpack on the seat of one of the chairs by a wood table some six feet from where Nicole stood. Nicole took a step in that direction, then stopped.

"Mr. King—"

"Jeff," he corrected.

"Jeff. I was wondering, could I give it to you tomorrow? I mean, I still have to study for your test, and you know Melanie took the best notes."

Sydney heard an echo in her mind: *She told me the trick to doing well in chemistry is to forget about the textbook and study the notes.*

"Sorry, Nicole," King was saying. "I need it now."

"Oh, well," she said brightly, "it never hurts to ask." She gestured toward the chair. "It's right over there. See?"

Sydney could tell Nicole was trying to maneuver King so his back would be to her, but he stood his ground.

If she tried to rush him now, he would see her well before she got close to him. All she had going for her was the element of surprise, and she didn't want to lose that if she could help it.

Nicole lifted the backpack from the chair and plopped it on the table with a thud. "Wait a minute . . . did I leave it at home?"

"Look for it."

Even from where Sydney hid, she could see Nicole's hands shaking as she fumbled with the zipper on the backpack.

"What's the matter, Nicole?" King asked.

"Nothing." She yanked at the zipper and it opened. She began to pull books and papers out, tossing them on the table. One skidded off to the floor. "Damn it."

King took a step closer to Nicole. Although his body was angled so Sydney couldn't see what it was, she saw him bring something out of his right jacket pocket.

The pen, she thought, her hand going to her own pocket. Better than nothing.

But it wasn't a pen he was holding, she saw by the startled expression on Nicole's face.

"What? Mr. King, what—"

"Call me Jeff," he said. "You are a very pretty girl, Nicole."

Sydney took a breath and slowly began to rise to a standing position, but carefully so he wouldn't hear her and turn.

"A very pretty girl," King repeated, "but not, I think, as innocent as you look."

Nicole tried to smile, but it faltered. "What are you talking about?"

"You know." He took another step. His right hand and whatever was in it were by his side.

One more step, Sydney thought. One more step and his back would be fully to her. He wouldn't see her coming, and he might not be able to turn in time . . .

"Here it is," Nicole said.

King partially blocked her view of Nicole, but she heard the sound of pages rustling.

"Give it to me."

Nicole held it out, but didn't move. "Here it is."

He took a step, and Sydney flew at him, hitting him a hard blow in the middle of his back with her shoulder. They both fell to the floor.

"Run, Nicole!"

Nicole dropped the notebook and started to run, but King grabbed at her ankle and she fell to her knees.

Sydney kicked him, her boot heel glancing off his knee, still trying to grab his right arm. "Get out of here, Nicole. God damn it, run!"

Nicole scrambled to her feet and made it to the door.

Sydney dug her nails into King's right wrist. She still couldn't see what he held in his hand, but she felt a hot slicing pain across the back of *her* hand.

He'd cut her.

She put one foot against his leg and pushed hard, wanting to get away from him before he could cut her again. The blood on her hand lubricated it, and she slipped from his hold.

She was on her knees, facing him as he staggered to his feet.

"She's going for help," Sydney breathed. "Give it up, King. You can't get away."

"I think I can." He wasn't even breathing hard. "We're the only ones on campus."

She got her feet under her and stood up. "What the hell are you talking about?"

"Didn't you know? All those questions you were asking? On Monday of finals week, they take all the girls for a night out. Relieves some of the tension." He smiled. "It's a Hilyer tradition, like letting loose the frogs."

He held his hand up, showing her a scalpel which had her blood on its blade.

"The same frogs I dissect in biology," he said and laughed.

"The police know you killed Melanie."

"Oh, do they?"

"Yes."

His eyes showed that he didn't believe her. "That's nice."

"Even if no one's on campus, Nicole will—"

"Nicole is locked out of every place but here. And this isn't a residential neighborhood, so if she's going for help, she's got a long way to run. I'll catch her." He smiled. "As soon as I'm through with you."

They were perhaps four feet apart, and he was between her and the door.

"You won't get away with this."

"Maybe I will."

She saw his muscles tense. The lab notebook Nicole had dropped was by her foot, and she kicked it toward him. When he looked down, she feinted to the left. Then ran to the right, away from the hand holding the scalpel.

He spun and slashed at her upper arm, but the denim jacket offered some protection and she barely felt it. She made it past him and hit the door at a full run.

It flew open and slammed against the facade of the building.

She knew her boots would slide if she tried to run down the steps, so she jumped all four of them, landed well and started across the grass.

He was right after her.

There was no time to think about evasion. She had to take the shortest way to the main building and the street beyond it.

Sydney ran through the trees near where Melanie had been murdered, her own breath loud in her ears. Where was Nicole? How long had it been?

She darted back and forth among the trees, hoping that he would not be as agile as she was, although he probably was faster. She heard him cussing.

Her foot caught on a tuft of grass and she pitched forward, but scrambled on all fours until she could stand upright again.

Just then, the sprinklers went on all around them. In only a few seconds, the grass became so slippery she fell again.

This time she felt a hand close around the ankle of her boot.

"Bitch," he said, and yanked on her leg.

She fell over onto her back and kicked out at his face. The heel of her boot caught him squarely in the chin, and even in the growing dusk she could see that she'd split the skin.

He lunged forward, the weight of his body knocking the air from her lungs.

She realized she still had the pen clenched in her hand and she used it to stab at his face, trying to catch him in the eyes.

She felt a cold pressure against her neck.

"Unless you want me to slit your throat," he breathed at her, "right here and now, you'd better—"

A scream came from a few feet away from them.

King looked up.

Sydney jammed the pen against the side of his head, thinking only to put him off balance; but she felt it strike something which gave a second later, and felt his hot blood pouring over her hand.

King collapsed on top of her.

The blade at her throat slid with his hand, but didn't cut deep.

"Sydney!"

She pushed at the dead weight of him, and he rolled off to one side. She sat halfway up, bracing herself on her elbows.

Water from the sprinklers splattered in her face as the cycle went around.

"Oh God." It was Nicole, and she fell to her knees beside Sydney.

The pen had gone into King's ear. Somehow in her desperation she had driven it deep, so hardly any of it could still be seen.

"God, you're bleeding."

"Nicole, did you call the police?"

As if in answer, she heard the first distant siren. She lay back down on the wet grass and waited for the cavalry to arrive.

EPILOGUE

Mitch Travis stood at the door to the office, nodding as a uniformed policeman talked. After a moment, the policeman left, and Mitch turned to her.

Sydney sat on the couch where Nicole had been slightly more than ninety-six hours before.

"What," he said, "is wrong with this picture?"

"How is Nicole?"

"She's fine. She doesn't look half as beat up as you do."

Sydney gave him a sarcastic smile. "Thanks."

He crossed the room and sat beside her. "You could have gotten killed, you know."

"Is he—"

Mitch nodded. "He died young and left a good-looking body."

She looked at him curiously. "Mitch, Victor said you were crediting me with breaking this case . . what is that all about?"

"Did I say that?"

"That's what I'm asking you."

"Hmm. You won't get mad, will you?"

"What?"

"I told him that to get him off my back. The son of a bitch can be a pain in the ass sometimes."

"So you sic him on me?"

"You're tough, kid. I knew you could handle him." He smiled and reached to brush her hair back from her face.

His fingers touched her cheek and she put her hand up to stop him. "I'm not that tough."

"I don't know. You got any more pens on you?"

"No." She picked a piece of wet grass off her jeans and twirled it between her thumb and forefinger. "So how did you know it was him?"

"Good solid police work. We ran a background check on all of the teachers. And of course their fingerprints are on file at the Department of Justice. We found out King had been fired from a job in Arizona after he'd been caught with one of his students in a compromising position."

"Uh huh."

"No charges were filed, because the girl's parents didn't want to put her through going to court and accusing him. His response had been that *she* had seduced him. I gather she wasn't a beauty like Melanie . . . there was a fair chance a jury—no doubt a female jury—would take a look at Superman and then at her and say, 'what would *he* want with *her*.'"

Sydney sighed. "The poor girl."

"She also said he'd given her drugs, and was even dealing them across the border. Nothing came of the allegation, but it set us thinking."

"Did Lillian Delacourt know? About his background?"

Mitch nodded. "She said something about good science teachers being hard to find."

"Right."

"Anyway, we were waiting at his place to pick him up."

"While he was here."

"Apparently so. We thought there was no one left on campus. We thought he was out with the rest of them, celebrating the end of the term."

"Except Nicole. She was here. Where was the librarian, Miss Shanfield?"

"She'd gone off with them. She says she asked Nicole if she wanted to come, but Nicole said no. She says she gave Nicole the keys and asked her to lock up."

That could well have been, Sydney thought. "Did you have a look at Melanie's notebook?"

"We did. She's got some formulas written in the back. Our guess is King may have been gearing up to try his hand at making drugs, instead of just dealing them."

"Cocaine?"

"Our chemist says no, it would be too hard. But crystal meth . . . heaven knows, there are meth labs all over San Diego county. We're the meth capital of the country."

"And he killed her for that? For the notebook?"

"He may have. We know they had a thing going for a while, hot and heavy. What ended it, I don't know."

The abortion? Sydney wondered.

"Regardless," Mitch continued, "she was going to turn him in. She was a bright girl, and she knew what he was doing, and when he walked away from her . . ."

Sydney could guess at the rest of it. "But the letter," she said. "Why kill her for her notebook when she'd written a letter which probably would have brought the heat anyway?"

"I don't think he knew about it. It was her safety net, insurance, in case he got his hands on the notebook. But he killed her before she could tell him."

"Has it turned up?"

"Not that I know of. We notified the newspapers to keep an eye out. But maybe it's somewhere, sitting in a stack of papers we haven't gone through yet. Anderson said she was a compulsive rewriter."

Sydney nodded.

They were silent for several minutes.

"Well," she said finally, "If you're through with me, I'd like to take Nicole home."

"I'm not. Through with you."

She glanced at him.

"We could get married, you know."

"What?"

"My divorce will be final in a couple of months."

"Mitch—"

318

"Think about it, Sydney."

She got up slowly and started for the door, but stopped before she reached it and turned. "Mitch, you know I love Ethan."

He smiled. "Maybe. But you *want* me."

She didn't answer him.

THE FINEST IN SUSPENSE!

THE URSA ULTIMATUM   (2130, $3.9)
by Terry Baxter

In the dead of night, twelve nuclear warheads are smuggled nort
across the Mexican border to be detonated simultaneously in ma
jor cities throughout the U.S. And only a small-town desert law
man stands between a face-less Russian superspy and World Wa
Three!

THE LAST ASSASSIN   (1989, $3.9)
by Daniel Easterman

From New York City to the Middle East, the devastating flames
revolution and terrorism sweep across a world gone mad . . . as th
most terrifying conspiracy in the history of mankind is born!

FLOWERS FROM BERLIN   (2060, $4.5)
by Noel Hynd

With the Earth on the brink of World War Two, the Third Reich
deadliest professional killer is dispatched on the most heinous a
signment of his murderous career: the assassination of Frankli
Delano Roosevelt!

THE BIG NEEDLE   (1921, $2.9)
by Ken Follett

All across Europe, innocent people are being terrorized, homes a
destroyed, and dead bodies have become an unnervingly commo
sight. And the horrors will continue until the most powerful orga
nization on Earth finds Chadwell Carstairs — and kills him!

DOMINATOR   (2118, $3.9)
by James Follett

Two extraordinary men, each driven by dangerously ambiguou
loyalties, play out the ultimate nuclear endgame miles above th
helpless planet — aboard a hijacked space shuttle called DOMINA
TOR!

*Available wherever paperbacks are sold, or order direct from th
Publisher. Send cover price plus 50¢ per copy for mailing and han
dling to Zebra Books, Dept. 2653, 475 Park Avenue South, Ne
York, N.Y. 10016. Residents of New York, New Jersey and Penn
sylvania must include sales tax. DO NOT SEND CASH.*